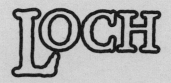

LOCH

No pictures, please.

The explosion from the water came quickly. What Erdon saw through the camera's lens was a shining mass of night erupting up toward him, a darkness hitting into him with such force he was airborne. The camera fell from his hands as he glimpsed a pair of huge, horrifying, yellow eyes and a gorge rimmed by jagged, dagger-sized teeth. The horror happened so fast—as if Erdon had been struck by the hood of a racing car, his feet torn from the rope webbing—he had but an instant to feel the impact on his face and chest. He was aware of a brief sensation of being turned, positioned, when a godless, fiery pain crashed simultaneously into his back and groin. Erdon's last conscious thought was the realization that he was being chewed in half.

LOCH

A NOVEL BY PAUL ZINDEL

Hyperion Paperbacks for Children

First Hyperion Paperback edition 1995

Text © 1994 by Paul Zindel

First published in hardcover in 1994. Reprinted by permission of Harper Collins Publishers.

3 5 7 9 10 8 6 4 2

Typography by Al Cetta.

Library of Congress Cataloging-in-Publication Data

Zindel, Paul.
Loch : a novel / by Paul Zindel. — 1st Hyperion Paperback ed.
p.   cm.
Summary: Fifteen-year-old Loch and his younger sister join their
father on a scientific expedition searching for enormous prehistoric
creatures sighted in a Vermont lake, but soon discover that the
expedition's leaders aren't interested in preserving the creatures.
Audience: Grades 6–12.
ISBN 0-7868-1099-8
[1. Underwater exploration—Fiction. 2. Monsters—Fiction.
3. Brothers and sisters—Fiction.] I. Title.
PZ7.Z647Lo   1995
[Fic]—dc20   95-8884

To my son, David Zindel,
whose encouragement was steady and unwavering.
My appreciation for his contributions—
and journeying with me to the Loch.

CONTENTS

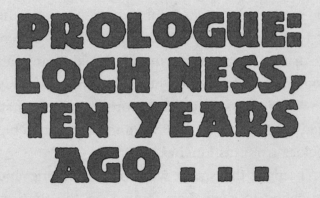

PROLOGUE: LOCH NESS, TEN YEARS AGO . . .

Luke Perkins watched his father light the camp-fire as his mother cleaned and prepared the trout, brushing each speckled fish with herbs and butter and securing it fast between the jaws of a metal rack. The boy had been told to stay near the Coleman lantern by the tent and to play with his pocket video game until dinner was ready, but he had long ago lost interest in the tiny electronic blips. The restless bleating of a herd of sheep nearing the edge of the loch was much more to his liking.

He was thankful his parents didn't see him as he wandered into the night, down the steep slope to the water. He knew they would have stopped him, shouting NO NO NO. His eyes widened with excitement when he saw the first of the sheep reach the deep, black waters to drink. Perhaps in moonlight the animals wouldn't run from him, he thought, not the way they had on sunny afternoons when he had tried to feed them M&Ms and chocolate-chip cookies from his lunches.

Tonight the sheep were busy drinking and struggling to keep their footing on the slippery slab of shore rock. The boy knew a great deal about these sheep and most of the living creatures of the loch, things he hadn't learned enough words to be able to tell anyone. He knew the sheep were afraid of the loch—in the same way that his mother and some of the other grown-ups were. He knew they believed there was something scary and not nice hiding in the water, something that was the stuff of bad

4

dreams. But he didn't feel their fear. Instead, he felt as he knew his father felt—excited by the smell of the night wind and the flash of a carp rolling near a log.

He reached the edge of the lake and froze like a bird dog next to the drinking herd. Finally, when he moved again toward the sheep, he was barely breathing, a trick he had learned when trying to surprise a rabbit or a quail. As more sheep arrived, they overflowed the first flank of animals. Several impatient ones darted behind the boy, and before he knew it, he was surrounded by the shifting animals.

He reached out to touch one, then another. At first he was thrilled by the feel and sharp smell of their damp, oily wool. The animals, driven by thirst, pressed closer, and the little boy became worried when one nudged him, causing his left sneaker to slip into the cold brim of the lake. He thought he had better call out to his mother and father, but quickly there was a splash to his right. He looked and saw that the herd had crowded two of the drinking sheep so badly, they had fallen, baaaaing, into the water. The two animals struggled to get back onto the steep, slippery shore, but neither could get a footing against the moonlit wall of the herd.

Suddenly there was a whooshing sound, and he watched, astonished to see one of the paddling sheep disappear from sight, yanked under the water like a fishing bob when a great bass has struck. The boy slipped farther. He struggled to push back against the herd, to get away from the edge. The second sheep bleated wildly now, confused, circling out into the deeper water as if hoping to find an unseen ledge. This time the child noticed the great wake, a profound undulation of the water heading for the desperate animal. Something dark and huge was coming, and when it struck, the white body of the sheep burst above the water. The eerie carcass shook and was propelled a dozen feet to the left, then back at a sharp angle. The boy heard the snapping and cracking. He glimpsed what he knew so many had been afraid of when they spoke of Loch Ness.

"Help! Help!" he screamed, fighting to break loose from the panicking herd. He kicked, slipped and fell, then managed to grab onto the branches of a thorny bush. Finally, he was on his feet again and clear of the animals. He saw his mother and father racing down the slope from the campfire. Soon they would reach him. He would tell them everything he had seen, though he knew they wouldn't believe him. But all that didn't matter, now that he was safe for tonight.

tucked again into some of the shadows. To the near boundary, then turned. In the middle of the loch a mottled-green form broke the surface with a faint crackle and an arch. There may have been three, there may have been two. Loch could not tell, for that he was sure he might.

THE HOUR OF THE BEAST

Loch turned away from the plunging mountain-
side until he floated hundreds of feet above
Lake Alban. He shifted his weight below the
aluminum-and-canvas wings, turning the hang
glider more sharply, circling. Even as the morning sun rose clear of the high ridges to the east,
the lake below remained peat-laden black and
grasped by the final, thin fingers of the dawn
fog.

Lake Alban was profoundly cold, a sixteenmile-long, narrow, and unspoiled lake in the rugged and sparsely populated highlands of Vermont. It had once been an arm of massive Lake Champlain to the west, carved to depths of over nine hundred feet by a mighty glacier knife. Lake Alban, like Loch Ness in Scotland, was abundant in salmon, eel, and other bottom feeders, food favorable in the eyes of a few scientists to the breeding of massive aquatic animals. But despite recent emotional TV interviews with eyewitnesses, other, more traditional scientists were only amused by tales of terrifying creatures imagined to live in remote waters.

Loch soared in his winged harness. He loved to lift the tip of the glider high above the horizon, let the glider stall, then free-fall until the wind rushed back under the wings to give him control again. He was fifteen now, a handsome, strong boy with shaggy, light-brown hair and deep-green eyes. He had changed a great deal in the years since Loch Ness, when he was the child who cried that he had seen a great water beast. Of course, his parents had smiled—somewhat nervously—and humored him about seeing the monster. It was the children from the town of Inverness who had giggled most and were the first to call him Loch.

The years had so clouded the memory of what had happened on that moonlit night that Loch himself spoke of it only as a childhood imagining. But there were two other events that made Loch's childhood seem many millions of light-years away. The first was the happy birth of his sister, Zaidee, who was now a handful and more than ready for the fifth grade. The second event was the sad and unthinkable death of his mother from leukemia only a year ago.

"She won't die," his father had assured him and Zaidee over and over again. "The chemotherapy is working, the marrow transplant is taking. No, your mother won't die."

But she did. On a snowy, chilling winter's day they had buried her in the family plot near a strip mine outside Star Lake, New York. Finally, now, they all accepted that she was gone forever.

The sky wind whipped Loch's shirt as he straightened out the flight of the glider high over the eastern tip of the lake. He started to raise the tip of the glider again but leveled out when he heard a plane approaching. The droning sound grew loud, then louder still, until it was earsplitting. Loch banked his glider in time to see the familiar Sea-B Amphibian burst from the towering white cloud above him. The sun exploded off the plane's fat, stainless-steel body and rear-drive propeller, blinding Loch for a moment. When he looked again, he saw his father's boss, Cavenger, at the controls. Cavenger's daughter, Sarah, was next to him, waving at Loch from the plane's outsized custom windows.

Loch had planned it like this, to be in the sky when Sarah arrived. He wanted her to see him soaring high, to show his pal how well he had learned to fly, and he was thrilled to see her smiling at him as the Sea-B circled. He quickly put his glider into a stall, then let it fall longer and faster than he had any right to.

The wind finally caught under Loch's wings again, as Cavenger dropped the Sea-B for an approach to the lake. The Amphibian came in low above the project's encampment, lording its roar over the heads of the hired crews readying the boats for the day's search. Loch knew the raucous maneuver was one more inspired gesture by Anthony Cavenger to remind all who worked for him: I pay you, I control you, I own you.

Gliding toward home base, Loch had judged the wind currents well. He scanned the desolate north shore of the lake, with its single dirt road to the old logging mill. He gave a last glance toward the massive blue basin to the west that was Lake Champlain, then glided down over the forest and smoking chimneys of the few homes that dotted the paved road south of Lake Alban. Several times in the past he had misjudged the morning convection drafts. He had fallen short and had to set his glider down on the little-traveled roadway. Today he knew he could easily make it to the field near his father's trailer. As he cleared the last patch of mist and a knoll of tall pines, he saw his sister waiting by the duck pond, waving him in.

Loch set the glider down and was out of its harness in time to catch Zaidee when she reached him. "You looked like a chicken hawk up there," she said, the strands of her bobbed hair bouncing up to her ears as she jumped. She locked her arms and swung from his neck. "When are you going to teach me to hang glide?" she asked, so wanting to be just like her big brother. "When?"

➤

"How long have you worked for Cavenger?" the young man wanted to know as he helped move boxes of research equipment from the back of the U-Haul truck into Sam Perkins's 1978 Volvo.

"About seven years," Sam answered, just to be polite about it. Small talk with college graduates just starting to claw their way up the corporate ladder had never been his strong point.

Erdon checked deeper inside the U-Haul truck. Most of the boxes were brimming with Sam's measurement gauges, core samplers, and other marine research equipment. "What's under the canvas?"

"An old Jet Ski." Sam grabbed the last box. "It huffs and puffs, but it still kicks water."

"Great." If there was one thing Erdon knew he'd need on this hick assignment, it would be some quality playtime. "Mind if I take it out on the lake sometime?" he asked. "I sort of grew up on one."

"No problem," Sam said, having no intention of ever really letting him borrow anything.

He had met dozens of self-conscious, muscled young men like Erdon, yuppies just out of school, thinking the world owed them a living.

"You went to U.C.L.A.?"

"Does it show?" Erdon asked defensively.

"Well, that's what it says on the decal you've got plastered on your Pathfinder."

"Oh."

Sam struggled to open the rear loading door of the Volvo station wagon. He was proud of the 193,000 miles he'd put on it, even as he used his old screwdriver trick to spring the broken hatch lock. Dr. Sam, as everyone called him, had become a highly respected marine biologist during the first dozen years he'd been out of Boston University. That all seemed very long ago to him now, long before he had married the bright and loving Joan Meisner and she had given him two wonderful children—and long before he'd gone to work for Cavenger. He didn't care that he looked shopworn in his dusty brown cap and big-pocketed fatigues, well frayed from the strong detergents of Laundromats.

"I was wondering how you made the transition from marine research to working for

Cavenger," Erdon said, putting his pair of Nikon cameras back around his neck. "I mean, my textbooks had half a dozen species of marine life carrying your name."

"It's called following the money," Sam said bluntly, surprised Erdon had done his homework. "Exactly what you're doing." He turned and headed for the trailer, with Erdon after him.

"Cavenger says you have photos, sketches of what we're looking for in the lake," Erdon pressed. "I mean, I'll be doing the stills and video, but if I could see what you've got, it might help me know what to expect. Was it Darwin or Pasteur who said chance favors the mind that's prepared?"

Dr. Sam was thankful to see Loch and Zaidee running up the knoll.

"It was great up there this morning, Dad," Loch said, breaking into a wide grin. "Saw clear across Lake Champlain."

"Good, son," Dr. Sam said. "Loch, this is Mr. Erdon. He's doing the documentary camera work on today's search. Give him the special Cook's tour, okay?"

"Sure," Loch agreed, smiling devilishly.

"My brother and I have a laptop we play

Crashers on," Zaidee bragged, as she pushed by everyone to be the first inside the trailer. "I'll show you after I go to the bathroom."

"Watch your head," Loch warned Erdon as they followed her inside. "Try not to step on the scuba masks."

Zaidee went into the john as Dr. Sam gave his son a wink and dropped into the dining nook to finish his long-cold morning coffee. "The main event's in my room," Loch told Erdon. He led him through the maze of furniture and lab equipment to the back of the trailer. "In there," Loch said, pointing to a door. Erdon reached out, opened the door, and started in. Suddenly, from out of the shadows, the head of a hideous beast, its mouth gaping, lunged down for Erdon's face.

"Ahhhhh!" Erdon screamed, his Nikons clanking as he threw up his arms. The head, its ferocious eyes glaring from a mass of matted hair, bounced off his elbow, snapped back, and came forward again and again in decreasing arcs.

"Sorry," Loch apologized, lighting up with a grin. He reached past Erdon and grabbed the fake monster head, which hung from a fishing string. Loch set the head back on top of a shelf. "It's just a little joke we play on visitors to our humble hall of cryptids."

Erdon's face was flushed, adrenaline pulsing through him as he heard Dr. Sam laughing in the dining nook. "It wouldn't be so funny if I had a heart condition," he called out angrily, trying to hide his embarrassment. Finally, he walked into the bedroom. Loch flicked on the light. Erdon's face moved slowly into a glow of astonishment. "Oh, my God," he said, his eyes scanning the blitz of shocking drawings, eerie photos, and models of dozens of grotesque creatures. "I've never seen anything like this." He took one of the Nikons and started shooting away. "What are they?"

Loch brushed a pile of science books and computer magazines from his bed onto the floor and sat down. "Just your average devil pig, water dragon, and Sasquatch," Loch said, ticked off that Erdon hadn't asked if he could take pictures. "Haven't you seen all the cryptozoo junk Cavenger stores at his London publishing offices?"

"I'm just playing catch-up. You know, my folks would never have let me keep my room like this," Erdon said enviously. "This is terrific." He reached out to touch the head of a tremendous, toothed skull. "My mom made me keep everything out of sight. She wrapped half our house in plastic."

Loch felt an ache in his stomach. He took the skull from Erdon. "This is a plaster head of a Tzuchinoko, a monster lots of people say they've seen around lakes," he said, wanting to move away from remembering how much he missed his own mother. If she were still alive, Loch knew, she would make certain Zaidee, Dr. Sam, and he lived in a much neater home too. "People claim it's a thick-bodied snake with twisted horns above its eyes."

"But it's all really a big crock," Erdon said, loud enough for Dr. Sam to hear him.

"Sure, it's probably a catfish brought to the top by a drought," Loch agreed, "but last year the town of Chigusa, Japan, believed in it enough to offer a two-million-yen reward for a living specimen. Cavenger had us off and running on that one too."

Erdon smirked. "You guys always find diddly, right?"

"Doesn't matter. Cavenger hypes it up into grist for his weird magazines, like *News of the Strange* and *Phenomena Monthly*. He had us search a year for a Waheela, this white wolf beast sighted in Canada."

Erdon shuffled through a stack of sketches of ferocious flying creatures and sea monsters, photographing everything that caught his eye. He knew he could easily freelance a couple of photo layouts to Cavenger's competitors. "Who did the drawings?"

"I do a lot of them," Loch said proudly.

"They're not bad." Erdon leaned across a cluttered table to get a closer look at a set of dark, shadowy photo enlargements thumb-tacked to the wall. "These are supposed to be of the Loch Ness monster, right?"

"The shot showing the big fin is the best," Loch said. "They call it the Ledniz shot."

Erdon knew that photo alone had been bought and reprinted so many times it had been an annuity for the photographer. "Lots of the photos have been shown to be phony. That one guy on his deathbed admitted his photo was a toy submarine, right?"

"All the photos can't be fakes," Loch said.

"Something like Nessie is what Cavenger thinks is in Lake Alban?"

"A few locals think so too."

From what Erdon had seen of the citizens of Lake Alban, he'd decided they'd invent anything to bring a few tourist bucks into the area. "What do they say?"

"Let me tell him!" Zaidee barged in, carrying the laptop and cornering Erdon. "Mrs. Mitchell who runs the grocery store said she saw a big black thing down near the fish grid. And Jesse Sanderson, who's the caretaker at the logging mill, said he saw something off his dock that had a head the size of a barrel, but everyone says he's a nasty, no-good pain-in-the-neck who drinks all the time. And a schoolteacher down the street said she saw two sets of fins twenty feet apart, and she thinks there's something in this lake that could hurt somebody a lot, a real lot. . . ."

The phone rang and Dr. Sam grabbed it. A moment later he called in to them. "There's a storm heading down from Canada. Cavenger wants the search under way immediately. Everybody to the dock. On the double!"

SOUNDS

Loch drove Dr. Sam and Zaidee in the Volvo. He'd already driven lots of times on expeditions, and now that he had turned fifteen, it was actually legal in Vermont for him to be behind the wheel. Erdon followed alone in his Pathfinder. "Can I turn on the radio?" Zaidee asked, reaching out for the shortwave.

"Sure," Dr. Sam said. "Just don't broadcast."

Zaidee hit a lot of static but finally tuned in a couple of boaters talking about fuel. She switched channels and picked up somebody giving a weather update to a guy with a French accent. Within minutes they had reached the main encampment and pulled into a parking area near Cavenger's Sea-B, which had been brought ashore and tethered.

The base was swarming with workers, boat crews, and research personnel rushing toward the army-style pontoon dock. Inflated rubber boats with outboards were taxiing the teams out to the lineup of motley skiffs anchored off-shore.

"What a mob scene," Erdon called to Dr. Sam as he got out of the Pathfinder. The Nikons around his neck clanked together, pop-ping one of the lens caps onto the ground.

Sure, because Cavenger hires too many butt-heads like you, Dr. Sam felt like shouting back, though he knew that wouldn't say much for himself, either. He had learned long ago that Cavenger's M.O. was to hire cheap, not good. Besides, when anyone finished negotiating a deal with Cavenger, he was lucky if he still had a nose left on his face.

"I can carry something else," Zaidee said, clutching the laptop.

"We got it," Dr. Sam said, taking the heavi-est box of equipment. Loch grabbed another container and they walked by Erdon, who was struggling to lift a commercial Panasonic video camera with a massive battery pack out of the back of the Pathfinder.

Loch took pity. "You need help?"

"No," Erdon said, stumbling.

"I still want to show you our Crashers game," Zaidee shouted to Erdon over the din of the crowd.

Erdon laughed. "I won't forget." He got a grip on the equipment and ran to catch up with the Perkins family.

When they reached the dock, Erdon stopped to roll up the sleeves of his shirt to better show off his build, then lugged the video camera and battery pack aboard his assigned boat—a powered catamaran specially designed for photography. The cat, which had first been rigged for one of Cavenger's Congo expeditions, was fitted with dual 190-horsepower Mercury outboards and an equalizing platform that minimized motor and wave interference to the cameras. The only other boat docked took up the lion's share of space: Cavenger's yacht, *The Revelation*.

Loch broke into a wide smile when he saw

Sarah waiting for him at the gangplank. "Hi, Sarah," he said.

"Hi." Sarah anxiously pulled at her curly, long brown hair so it fell forward down the sides of her face.

"Did you see me doing stalls on the glider?"

"Of course I saw you," Sarah said. Her platform shoes made clopping sounds when she shifted from one foot to the other.

Zaidee spoke up, staring at Sarah's feet like they were gremlins. "Nice footwear for boating."

"Oh, hi, Zaidee," Sarah said. She tried to sound enthusiastic about seeing her again, but she found Zaidee getting more and more on her nerves the older she got. "All my friends in London are wearing platforms. They're really more comfortable than they look."

Zaidee looked straight into Sarah's eyes. "You've got to be kidding."

"I'll catch up with you," Loch told Zaidee.

"I get the point. I'm being banished. Big deal," Zaidee said, continuing up the gangplank.

Loch set the box down and smiled at Sarah. "Did your mom come with you?"

"No. You know she hates Dad's expeditions. Why didn't you answer my last letter?"
she asked. "I wrote you seven months ago!"
She didn't mean to sound so whiny, but she
needed words to hide her nervousness. She was
thrown to see he had the start of a mustache
and even a shadow of a beard. "You've gotten
bigger."

"So have you," Loch said without thinking.
He didn't mean to be looking at her body when
the words came out, and he knew she had
caught him. "I was going to write," Loch went
on, "but then I kept thinking I was going to see
you." He meant it, but there was something
about putting a pen to paper that was really
painful. The pen could never keep up with his
thoughts.

"All I know is I'm sure the questions were
urgent for me when I wrote them, and now I
suppose it doesn't matter at all," Sarah said.
She could tell from the look in his eyes that he'd
had enough of her bellyaching.

"Well, I guess I'd better get this on your
dad's boat," Loch said, picking up the container
again.

"Yes, I guess you'd better. See you around,"

Sarah said, clopping away from *The Revelation*, heading across the dock.

"Hey, where are you going?" Loch asked, puzzled.

"Dad said I can drive the catamaran today," she called over her shoulder. Erdon was waiting for her on the cat. All smiles, he reached out to help her aboard.

Loch watched her get behind the controls. He knew she was just pulling rank as the boss's daughter, but that wasn't anything new. He took his shirt off, then set the container on his left knee to get a better grip. He caught Sarah staring at him from the cat, gave her a wave, then boarded the yacht. A deckhand helped him store the gear, and he caught up to Zaidee sitting on the rear lounge deck. She had the laptop open and was mesmerized by Crashers.

"Sarah looks different, don't you think?" Loch asked.

"She wants to jump your bones," Zaidee said without looking up.

Loch laughed. "I wish," he said, tousling her hair and swinging up into his favorite hiding spot, the yacht's rubber raft, the one used to get to shore in shallow bays. The one thing Zaidee and he had learned a long time ago was to keep out of sight until a search got under way.

>➤

"You're late again!" Cavenger glared from the control console. "We've started the sonar check."

"Sorry," Dr. Sam said, sliding into his seat at the recorders.

"Are the trawler nets ready?" Cavenger demanded to know.

"Yes sir," Randolph, a radio specialist, said quickly.

"Tell the fleet to start engines!" Cavenger shot the order out as he stood up to check the port and starboard flanks.

"Start engines!" Emilio, Cavenger's head troubleshooter, passed the command.

The simultaneous roar from the engines of the yacht and fourteen skiffs echoed off the mountainsides. Cavenger yanked the microphone out of Emilio's hand. "Low idle!" he yelled. The tumult from the engines dropped quickly.

He handed the mike back to Emilio. "I want to go in sixty seconds," Cavenger said as he sat his thin, frail body back down in the black-leather swivel chair. With bald head and sunken eyes, he looked ghostly in the flickering of the sonar screens. Emilio, short, stocky, in his forties, sat on Cavenger's right. On his left was John Randolph, a retired Air Force pilot and radioman. Haskell, the ship's captain, was at the wheel. Behind them all, out of the power loop, was Dr. Sam, adjusting the styluses on the sonar graphic recorders.

The clanking sounds from the pair of shabby old brown fishing trawlers stabbed through the air as they flanked the fleet. Both trawlers were already in motion as planned, with a dozen Portuguese fishermen feeding out hemp netting from huge, rusted spindles.

"Are you ready, Sam?" Cavenger demanded to know.

"Ready," Dr. Sam said.

Emilio looked at Cavenger.

"Go!" Cavenger ordered.

The water in the bay churned as the engines kicked their strength into the string of propellers. The boats lunged forward, shooting back trails of the peat-black deeper waters toward the shore.

"The line's scraggly!" Cavenger complained.

Randolph snapped to and took to the open deck with a power megaphone.

"Stay back of our bow!" he called off the port, then starboard, reinforcing the command with arm signals. The experienced skippers quickly firmed the lines until the boats looked like a wedge of flying geese, with *The Revelation* in the lead.

"Stay under seven knots if you want maximum sonar density," Dr. Sam reminded.

The only boat to break the line was the catamaran. Loch swung down from the raft to watch Sarah circling *The Revelation*. She throttled the dual giant outboards of the cat, forcing Erdon to hold on to the video mount for support. Emilio moved out onto the open deck of the yacht to glare at her. She slowed down fast, allowing Erdon to get on with his shoot. Sarah saw Loch watching, let out a yelp, and gave him a big wave.

Zaidee looked up from Crashers and saw Sarah showing off. "Puberty must really suck," she muttered.

Ten minutes into the search, Loch and Zaidee knew it was safe to make the transition from the rear deck to the control room, where they could watch Dr. Sam work. Once a search was under way, Cavenger and his crew were always much too busy even to notice them. As they entered the control room, the ocean of lighted dials and the BLIP . . . BLIP . . . BLIP of the monitor screens were hypnotic. Zaidee gave a thumbs-up to her dad and snuggled into a chair by the door. Loch moved farther into the room and slipped onto the seat next to his dad.

"Hi," Loch whispered.

Dr. Sam gave them both a wink, then dropped his stare back onto the graphic recorders. The dozen styluses scratched ink zigzags on the rolls of graph paper marching forward beneath them, a permanent record of the lake floor and everything in between.

"I want the nets full out." Cavenger snapped his fingers. Randolph broadcast the order to both trawlers.

"I told you to use steel netting," Dr. Sam reminded Cavenger.

"Too expensive," Cavenger shot back.

"Not if we find what you're looking for."

"Suppose I worry about that, Sam," Cavenger said coldly, reaching his skinny hand to his neck, checking his shirt collar.

"If it's any type of plesiosaur, it's going to have teeth," Dr. Sam said.

"You underestimate what fifteen million years of evolution, trapped in a lake like this, can do to an animal," Cavenger said. "The same goes for whatever's in Loch Ness, and that cousin of Nessie's they've been spotting in British Columbia. Somebody's going to catch one soon, and you'll see what happens when you cramp any kind of beast long enough. It's not going to evolve. A trapped beast devolves, it goes down the ladder of evolution. Like you, Sam," Cavenger said, laughing.

Loch's fingers tightened into a fist. He hated it when Cavenger put his father down in front of everyone, and he did that a lot. Maybe what Loch hated most was the way his father just took the abuse.

"You're right about that, Mr. Cavenger." Randolph backed Cavenger up as usual. By now he knew Cavenger's every pet theory like a catechism. "It's what happened to the sturgeon, right?"

"You bet it is." Cavenger nodded. "Sturgeons were killers of the seas. A few million years trapped in glacial freshwater, and what do they end up as—pole fish with a suctorial, toothless mouth. Anything we find in this lake will be lucky if it doesn't have to drink its food through a straw!"

Loch wasn't going to sit still and let that one go by. "My dad and I catch a lot of northern pike with teeth as big as a barracuda's." Dr. Sam knocked his son with his knee as Cavenger swiveled in his chair. His nasty little eyes glared at Loch; then he chuckled, saying to the others, "Like father, like son."

"And like father, like *daughter*," Zaidee spoke up from the back, as ticked off as Loch. She threw open the laptop and started playing Crashers again.

"We've got something," Cavenger cut in, his eyes back on the master screen in front of him.

Emilio squirmed in his seat. "Something large, submerged, at two o'clock."

"It's alive," Cavenger said.

Dr. Sam checked the zigzags, then glanced over to the sonar screens to confirm his reading. "No, it's not. It's a log."

"How do you know?" Cavenger asked condescendingly.

"Because I'm trained to read sonar, and because the old logging mill's dead off Boat Fourteen's starboard," Dr. Sam replied.

Randolph turned from the radio board. "Boat Fourteen reports eye contact. Confirms it's a log." Loch smiled and hit his father a silent high five as Cavenger stood and looked out toward the shore. "What's a goddam logging mill doing on this lake anyway?"

"There used to be a water flow out the west end, a river that flowed down to Lake Champlain," Randolph said.

"A deep river?" Cavenger wanted to know.

"Yes, pretty deep." Emilio spoke up. "But they've installed a salmon grid on it now. Works like a dam."

"They built the grid last year," Dr. Sam offered.

"That's why the thing is here then," Cavenger said, excited.

At the wheel, Captain Haskell looked puzzled. He had learned over the years that as far as Anthony Cavenger was concerned, it was better not to draw him out on much. But his curiosity got the better of him. "What thing? Why is what here?"

Cavenger smiled. "It's trapped. Our little creature is trapped."

AT THE TIME HORIZON

The north sky filled with dark clouds as the storm front marched over the mountain ridge. Just past the midpoint of the lake, the sonar picked up a surface disturbance in front of Boat One. The signal indicated something large and moving. As the boat closed, a cluster of swimming beavers was sighted. The beavers smacked the surface of the water with their tails and dove beneath the surface, splintering the signal.

The west end of the lake came into sight, and Loch went out on deck for a breath of fresh air. He didn't like to be around Cavenger when one of his elaborate electronic searches ended in abject failure, as, of course, they usually did. At those times, Cavenger became even more despotic and cruel. He'd slowly coil like a rattlesnake, his eyes growing dead as if he were looking inward at his own pathetic soul. Then, without warning, he'd strike out at any-one, and he usually picked Dr. Sam.

Loch waved again to Sarah on the catama-ran. He didn't like the way Erdon kept flashing his big smile at her and showing off his build. The wind had picked up and the surface of the lake began to ripple with small, white-capped waves. Sarah smiled, waved back, and throttled the engines like she was having the time of her life with Erdon. Loch found himself wishing he was the one on the cat with her, not some show-off with a couple of Nikons. Sarah and he had grown up together on Cavenger's expedi-tions. They saw each other no more than a cou-ple of months out of every year, but they had parasailed, swum with manta rays.

"Loch!" Zaidee called from the control-room doorway. "There's something wrong with Crashers!"

Loch went back inside and sat down with Zaidee. The picture on the laptop screen was of an iridescent forest and a frozen crystal river with a path leading across it. The cartoon figure of a young boy was being stalked by a hideous witch with a knife.

"Hey, congratulations!" Loch said. "You got to the fifth screen!"

"Yeah, but look at the squiggles," Zaidee complained, pointing to two thick black lines dancing across the middle of the screen.

"Probably interference from the sonar."

"It was okay before."

"Then maybe it's the storm coming," Loch said.

Zaidee took the laptop, shut it off, and flipped it closed. "I'll never get to the fifth screen by myself again."

Scratch . . . scraaatch . . .

Loch looked up. He saw his father tense, then lean forward to the graphic recorders. Loch too had detected the change in the pitch and rhythm of the styluses. He quickly moved next to his father.

"I'm showing something," Dr. Sam said.

Cavenger turned, his profile eerie in the light from the sonar screens. "I've got it too."

"It's reading as a large, moving object," Dr. Sam specified. Loch heard a rare tremor crawl into his father's voice.

"Other boats are radioing in," Randolph said, lifting half his headset.

"Tell them we've got it," Cavenger ordered. "Tell them to hold course and maintain speed."

"Whatever it is, it's alive. And deep," Dr. Sam said.

"As long as it stays in front of us," Cavenger said. He snapped his fingers at Emilio. "How far to the end of the lake?"

Emilio checked his map. "Less than a mile."

"Where is it now?" Cavenger demanded, his eyes dropping to the master screen.

"Still in front," Dr. Sam said.

Cavenger's hands began to shake. "Tell the trawlers to draw the nets!"

"Draw the nets!" Randolph yelled into the radio mike.

Loch ran out onto the deck, with Zaidee right after him. The storm was mounting quickly now, like a great black glove reaching across the mountains. The wind whipped the waves higher until they struck noisily at the sides of the boats. There was a flash of lightning, followed a few seconds later by a tremendous thunderclap. The crew worked to secure the deck furniture and roll up the flapping awnings.

"Think it's something real this time?" Zaidee asked, looking anxiously into her brother's eyes.

"Yes, I think it's real," Loch said softly.

➤

There was no sonar or radio on the catamaran. A great, black thunderhead loomed in the sky above, and Sarah took a couple of yellow rain slickers from the storage bin. She tossed one to Erdon, who was forward at the camera mounts.

"Thanks," he said, catching it. He forced a smile as he put the slicker on, but he didn't like the look of the thunderhead at all. He knew that a lake during a thunderstorm was not exactly the safest place to be.

Loch rushed to the bow of the yacht, with Zaidee after him. Ahead, he saw the deep undulation in the water, a sight he'd seen only once before. A chill moved across his chest as he remembered when he was a small boy standing at the edge of another dark, even deeper lake. He remembered the sounds of the sheep, their urgent bleating. . . .

Sarah and Erdon saw Loch and Zaidee signaling to them.

"What do they want?" Erdon called nervously over the slap of waves hitting the catamaran.

"I don't know," Sarah said, but she was certain they looked worried. Loch kept pointing ahead, toward the approaching shore.

"Maybe they found something," Erdon said. He felt goose bumps rise on his arms beneath the slicker.

"Maybe." Sarah saw the two trawlers crank up speed and pull ahead. "They're closing the nets!" she shouted, throwing the throttle forward, propelling the cat out in front.

"NO!" Loch yelled from the deck of *The Revelation.* He had wanted to signal Sarah about the radar showing something ahead, that she should stay back, closer to the protection of the yacht and fleet, but she didn't understand.

"Get the camera going!" she shouted to Erdon. The vibrations had loosened one of the leads from the battery pack, and it sparked until

Erdon tightened it. He put his eye to the viewfinder, turned the camera on, and pressed the RECORD button. The automatic focus whirred the lens forward and back, seeking a target.

The lake floor rose sharply now, the peat-black water turning to gray as the thick steel rises of the salmon grid stood like sentinels at the end of the lake. Sarah slowed the cat's engines as Cavenger ordered the fleet to cut power and hang back in neutral. Only the trawlers chugged ahead at full speed, straining to close the semicircle of their nets as quickly as possible—but they were too late. Something had gotten past them and was now between the shore and the nets.

Cavenger was on deck with the megaphone.

"There!" he shouted, pointing. "It's trapped!"

Sarah turned the cat to follow her father's directions as Erdon swiveled the video camera around on its mount. Through the camera's eye he saw a patch of water beyond the net begin to boil. Finally, the thing turned away from the shore. It looked as if it were going to try to escape through the nets back to the deep of the lake. Sarah watched, startled to see the net buoys tugged violently to the left.

"We're too close," she yelled.

"Shut the engines," Erdon shouted, a rush of panic filling his voice. "They're spooking it."

Sarah turned the ignition off, but the thing still battled against the net, shaking it. Suddenly, there was a great tearing, a snapping of ropes as the buoys sprang loose and the blackness submerged again.

"What's going on?" Erdon asked, confused. "What is that thing?"

Cavenger stood speechless, furious at the thought that the creature had escaped back toward the deep of the lake. Dr. Sam came out on deck. Zaidee ran to him, taking his hand. The crews on the drifting skiffs watched silently, waiting for Cavenger's next command.

Emilio rushed toward the bow from the control room. "Mr. Cavenger," he called, *"there's another one on the screen now!"*

"Probably the same one," Randolph muttered.

Emilio hesitated but finally got the words out. "No. This one's bigger. Much bigger."

"Where is it?" Cavenger asked.

"It's heading toward us."

Emilio dashed back into the control room with Cavenger and Randolph right after him. Dr. Sam took Zaidee with him.

Loch looked toward Sarah. He shouted across to the catamaran. "There's another one! Get the cat to shore!"

Sarah heard his warning and reached for the starter key.

"Don't," Erdon said, holding tightly to the camera mount for support. "We're better off staying still."

CRASH. Another tremendous thunderclap, and rain began to fall. Sarah stared down at the water behind the cat's outboards. Despite the rain, she slid her yellow slicker off. It made her feel too much like an outsized, glowing lure. Erdon followed her lead.

She froze when she saw the shadow fill the space beneath the catamaran.

"It's here!" she called out to Loch. The line of silent crews aboard the skiffs heard her too, but didn't move.

"I feel something," Erdon said.

Sarah nodded. She did too.

The cat was vibrating, turning slowly.

"It's touching us," Erdon said, barely audible. He began to curse himself for having signed on to the expedition in the first place.

There was a clearing in the peat of the water, an underwater spring rushing upward to dilute the blackness. Sarah's eyes widened in terror when she glimpsed the knobby scales of a spine and a pair of monstrous ribbed fins churning the water slowly, powerfully. . . .

Oh, it can't be, I can't be seeing this, Sarah told herself.

"Maybe it's some kind of whale," Erdon said, knowing he was lying even to himself. "The lakes and rivers are deep enough. Maybe pollution knocked out its navigation system. It could have made its way from the St. Lawrence to Champlain, then up here."

Sarah didn't lift her eyes from the water. "I don't think so."

"It could be some kind of manatee," Erdon said weakly.

"Shhhhh. It's listening for us," Sarah said softly.

After a moment the boat stopped its shaking. The mass of bony spine began to sink, fade into the darkness below.

"What's going on?" Erdon asked. "I can't see."

"It's leaving," Sarah said, watching the shadow sink deeper, then disappear altogether.

"You sure?" Erdon asked, stepping around the camera mount. He moved closer to the edge of the catamaran, angling himself to avoid the glare of the water's surface. He saw nothing and breathed a sigh of relief. "That was bigger than a bread box." He laughed nervously. He looked toward *The Revelation* and the fleet. "It's okay," he yelled. "It's gone. It was some kind of whale."

"Did you get it on camera?" Sarah asked.

"Just some shadows," Erdon said. He looked toward the yacht. Realizing he'd better at least put on a show for Cavenger, he grabbed one of his Nikons, the one with the fastest film, and stepped out on the left pontoon of the cat. Now he could appear brave. He sat down, straddling the bow like he was riding a horse. He figured he'd take some shots. Cavenger wouldn't have to know he had been too scared even to think about taking stills when the creature was under the boat. Now that there was no danger, he began to regret he hadn't gotten at least a shot of the spine or fins. If it had been some sort of prehistoric beast, he knew, his career as a marine photographer would have been made.

"Be careful," Sarah warned.

"No problem." Erdon smiled. He lay down on the bow, hooked his feet under the rope webbing at the front, and moved his torso out over the bow.

The explosion from the water came quickly. What Erdon saw through the camera's lens was a shining mass of night erupting up toward him, a darkness hitting into him with such force he was airborne. The camera fell from his hands as he glimpsed a pair of huge, horrifying, yellow eyes and a gorge rimmed by jagged, dagger-sized teeth. The horror happened so fast—as if Erdon had been struck by the hood of a racing car, his feet torn from the rope webbing—he had but an instant to feel the impact on his face and chest. He was aware of a brief sensation of being turned, positioned, when a godless, fiery pain crashed simultaneously into his back and groin. Erdon's last conscious thought was the realization that he was being chewed in half.

At first, Sarah didn't have time to scream. The gnarled, grotesque body of the beast hit the catamaran, knocking it upward and throwing her across the deck. Her body slapped against the outboards, then spilled like a rag doll into the recess behind the windshield. The cat and the creature dropped back down like falling stones, with a tremendous splash of water erupting around her. Instinctively, she reached for the ignition key, but as her arm and hand went out she felt the warm, thick drops spotting her skin. When she looked at her arm, she knew it was raining blood. Now she could scream.

Emilio and Dr. Sam were on the deck of the yacht yelling to Sarah. Cavenger had Haskell start the engines. He bolted from the control room with the megaphone, his voice roaring incomprehensibly toward his shrieking daughter.

Loch ran for the raft at the rear of the yacht and swung its cradle out over the water. He leaped in and threw the pulley release, and the raft splashed down. Loch yanked the start cord, the outboard roared to life, and he shot off toward Sarah and the beast. Off the cat's starboard, he had to swerve sharply to avoid a floating tree limb. As he passed it, he saw it was one of Erdon's legs.

The creature crashed upward from the surface again. It tilted its head back on its long, scaly neck, then snapped forward with its gaping mouth to tear into the wood of the catamaran. In a great splintering, the front half of the left pontoon fell away. The beast pulled its head back and struck again and again, then slowly sank once more under the water.

Sarah dragged her body across the shattered deck, as Loch rammed the rubber raft up onto the back of the sinking cat. "Get in," he yelled to Sarah as he gassed the engine, trying to hold the raft in position.

Loch saw the deep motion of the water. By now, Sarah, too, knew what that meant.

Before Sarah could get into the raft, the monstrous head of the beast erupted between them, throwing Loch and the raft into the air as Sarah fell forward to the camera mount. The neck of the creature continued to erupt upward, a tremendous, glistening shaft. High above, its head poised for a moment, the two great wedges that were its eyes stared down at the catamaran. The mouth of the beast opened and plunged down like a tremendous shredder. CRACK. CRACK. Its teeth tore into the back of the cat as Sarah began to slide down toward the gaping mouth.

"Help us!" Sarah screamed at the closest skiff. "Help . . ."

The jaws of the beast opened wider now. It roared a blast of stinking breath and shredded human intestines at Sarah as her right ankle got caught between the crushed engines. Only when the creature's teeth crashed into the outboards did it halt, then sink back again beneath the surface.

Loch had been knocked twenty feet from the stalled rubber raft. He started swimming for it, kicking for all he was worth. When he reached the raft, he hurled himself aboard it, but the motor wouldn't start. He dropped onto his stomach, swung his arms over the side of the raft, and dug into the water.

"Hurry!" Sarah called to him. "My foot is caught!"

"Hold on," Loch yelled.

They saw the creature's head surface on the lake. Only its snout and hooded, yellow, glaring eyes were coming at them now, gaining speed. It moved toward them like a massive, hungry crocodile. Finally, Loch reached Sarah with the raft, but her foot was still wedged between the engines. They both could see and smell gasoline as it spilled from the ruptured tanks and floated out into a widening slick.

"The cat's going down!" she cried.

Loch threw his shoulder against one of the engines as Sarah pounded her fists on the other. There was the crackling sound of sparks, and they looked to see that Erdon's battery pack had slid down the deck. It inched closer and closer to the gasoline.

Desperately, Loch tore off an engine cover and plunged his hand into the grease of the engine. He reached below the water for Sarah's ankle and thrust the grease onto her skin and the crushing metal. The creature was closing fast. Her foot slipped free.

"Get us out of here!" Sarah pleaded.

Loch pulled at the cord of the raft's outboard, but the motor still wouldn't start. The creature lifted its snout. The tremendous teeth of its upper jaw lifted into a deadly canopy as water rushed into the mouth.

"It's going to swallow us alive," Sarah screamed as she pulled herself into the raft.

The beast's mouth was fully open now, its

lower jaw distended. Loch gave a last desperate pull on the start cord and the motor screamed to life. When the hideous jaws snapped closed, they crashed onto the cat and the battery pack sparked for a last time. Loch and Sarah were racing toward *The Revelation* when the great explosion came.

WATERFALL

"I regret the death of the young photographer, but anyone who leaks any information about the incident will no longer be employed by this company," Cavenger said that night, moving for as much containment at the base as possible. "Within three or four days we'll be properly equipped to capture one of the beasts. Bonus incentives will be posted so each of you will enthusiastically complete your work on this expedition." Those who hadn't known Cavenger well realized by the end of the meeting that his physical frailty masked—from the unsuspecting—his complete ruthlessness.

Loch couldn't sleep that night. He lay awake with images of the monster crashing up from the water, its massive jaws and teeth hurtling down upon the catamaran. The ultimate moment of horror, Erdon being torn to pieces, played over and over in his mind. Loch couldn't think of a death more horrible. No one deserved to die like that. No one.

"Noooo . . . nooooo . . ." Zaidee cried out in her sleep.

Zaidee had made sounds when she dreamed for as long as Loch could remember. The year before, when their mother had died, Zaidee had gone through a sleepwalking phase. He would hear a noise and wake up to see Zaidee standing at his doorway, uttering strange words, as though speaking in tongues, not knowing where she was. Dr. Sam had told him never to wake her in the middle of a sleepwalk, just to put his arm around her and guide her back to her bed.

Loch got up in the dark, made his way past the clutter of cryptids, and went to Zaidee's room. He knelt down by her sleeping bag. When she cried out again, he shook her.

"Hey, it's a dream," Loch said, "a dream."

Zaidee flung her eyes open and stared at her

brother. "I wasn't having a dream," she said, rubbing her eyes. "I was having a nightmare . . . the worst nightmare in the world with a lot of bats landing on my face . . . and they were all trying to drink out of my mouth . . . and do other horrible things . . ."

"That wasn't nice of them, was it?" Loch said softly. He put his hand gently on her forehead. He remembered his mother used to do that when Zaidee had had a bad dream. "Zaidee," he said gently, "you saw what happened to Erdon. Maybe you want to sit up and talk about it. Sometimes it's better to talk about things. . . ."

Zaidee pulled the blanket up to her shoulders and turned over. "Lots of sauce on that pizza . . . a lot of sauce . . ." she muttered, and was asleep again.

➤

At breakfast, Dr. Sam gave each of his kids a hug. His only way to deal with what had happened on the lake was to push the images down deep, to bury them until he had time to deal with the tremendous rush of guilt he had felt over the attack on the lake. He had tried to raise Loch and Zaidee to be brave and not afraid of life, but he had never meant to put either of them in danger. He had lost his wife. If he lost Loch or Zaidee, he knew it would be more than he could survive.

"New rules," Dr. Sam announced.

"Here it comes." Zaidee rolled her eyes.

"Neither of you is to go out on the lake," Dr. Sam started. "I don't want you using our bass boat at the dock. Leave the Jet Ski in the U-Haul. If you want to fish, it's got to be from the shore. You can play catch, video games, and board games." Then he added, "I don't want either of you down at the main base when Cavenger hauls in the equipment for the next sweep."

"Okay," Loch and Zaidee said together, like they had rehearsed it.

"And it wouldn't hurt if you did a little schoolwork, either," Dr. Sam said, grabbing the Volvo keys.

"We did a lot of math last week," Loch said.

"Then help Zaidee with her spelling," Dr. Sam suggested. "Work on her vocabulary."

"We've done a lot of vocabulary," Loch insisted.

Dr. Sam stepped over the junk on the

floor. Loch looked at the mess and thought of Erdon's mom, who had always kept his room neat and the house half wrapped in plastic. "Did Cavenger call Erdon's family yet?"

"No," Dr. Sam admitted, taking a last sip of his morning coffee.

"That really sucks," Loch said.

"They'll know by tonight."

Zaidee gave her father a hug. "Daddy, how can you stand working for a man who's got three balls and the heart of a vulture?" She enjoyed shocking her father from time to time.

Dr. Sam choked on his coffee. "Zaidee, where did you hear that expression?"

"What expression?" Zaidee smiled, then looked at her brother.

Dr. Sam frowned at Loch, but Zaidee took her father's hand. "Don't worry, Daddy. We'll behave."

➤

Cavenger cashed in every government chip he had, calling politicians in half of New England. Larger craft were coming overland from the Coast Guard base in Groton, Connecticut. Woods Hole had agreed to send a couple of men specially trained in the handling of large ocean mammals. Metal netting was bought in Providence.

No one knew how many of the creatures there were. The first, smaller one was believed to be a female and, for purposes of the hunt, had been named Beast. The second, the one that had killed Erdon and was seen to survive the catamaran explosion, was designated the Rogue. Dr. Sam warned Cavenger there might be still more of the creatures in the lake. He explained his theory that the creatures had come from the 435-square-mile water basin that was Lake Champlain, that they had followed a spring salmon run up the deep river to Lake Alban, and that they had been trapped when the salmon grid went in. The only other possible point of origin for creatures their size would have been a journey starting from Lake George, which fed Lake Champlain. Dr. Sam's father had often taken him fishing on Lake George when he was a kid. He knew there were tremendously deep coves and bays that were as desolate and unfathomed as when Samuel de Champlain had first mapped the area in 1603. There was even the remote possibility that somewhere in Lake Champlain a sizable group of these creatures could be living in a highly developed social order.

"The one thing certain," Dr. Sam told Cavenger, "is that from the bite marks on the cat, and from what I saw of their jaw structure, they're a species of highly evolved plesiosaur, water beasts thought to have been extinct for over ten million years." He couldn't resist adding, *"Cap'n, this ain't no sturgeon."*

➤

Sarah woke in her room on the yacht, got out of bed, and staggered to look in the bathroom mirror. There were a few scratches on the left side of her face. A bump above her left eye had started to go down.

Not too bad, she thought, but she felt like she'd been run over by a juggernaut.

The morning light blasted in through the portholes of her cabin, and with it stirred all of what she had repressed about the attack. The memory of Erdon's red blood raining down onto her began to intrude, but she decided to think of something she could deal with. That was a trick of surviving she'd learned a long time ago. Keep the unpleasant parts of life away, always replace them with thoughts of

things you want to remember. This morning
she thought of Loch's deep-green eyes as he
had skimmed toward her in the raft.

Loch waited until Dr. Sam had left for the
base before he called Sarah. Cavenger had always let Sarah have her own private cellular
phone. Loch remembered their first silly date,
in London when they were eight years old. Dr.
Sam had brought Loch with him to London for
meetings with Cavenger. Sarah had a crush on
Loch and had wanted to go out for an ice
cream soda. Cavenger thought it would be fun
to have Sarah take his chauffeured white stretch
limo. She had her personal phone that afternoon, and ever since.

"What?" Sarah answered.

"Hi," Loch said. "Did I wake you up?"

Sarah was glad to hear his voice, in spite of
her pounding headache. "No." She rubbed her
head trying to get blood up to her brain.

"How do you feel?"

"Rotten. How about you?"

"I'm okay," Loch said. "I was just wondering if you had wheels and wanted to hang out
later."

Sarah climbed back under the covers with

the phone. "Loch," she said, "I need a day off. I haven't felt this whacked out since we were in that truck crash in Guatemala."

"The truck only fell on its side," Loch reminded her.

"To me that's a crash."

Loch could hear she was really drained. "All right," he said. "I'll check on you later, okay?"

"Thanks," she said. Then she remembered something. "Loch?"

"Yep?"

"Thanks for—"

"Hey, no problem," Loch said.

➤

By noon there wasn't a cloud in the sky. Loch and Zaidee decided to cast spinner and spoon lures off the old dock near the trailer. Nothing decent was biting. The only action they saw was from small sunfish who were furious the lures were sputtering through their underwater mud beds.

"My arm hurts," Zaidee complained, trying to find a new grip on her rod.

"Mine too," Loch admitted. He looked toward the deep water. "We know there's got to be some great salmon or trout out there."

Neither of them could help eyeing their bass boat tied up at the dock. It drifted back and forth in half circles, knocking gently against the rubber tires lining the pilings.

"We could take the boat out and stay in the shallows," Zaidee said. "We'd be safe—the water's really clear there."

"Let's not, and say we did," Loch suggested, his long shaggy hair covering his brow now. Zaidee switched to a heavier spinner, casting it as far out as she could. No matter how she tried, it always fell short of the black water where the shallows gave way and the bottom fell sharply into the great trench of the lake.

"We could just stay along the shoreline," Zaidee said. "There are shallows all the way up to the salmon grid. Imagine the size of the fish up there. Fish always hang out at a dam."

"We told Dad we wouldn't," Loch said.

"We'll be safe," Zaidee insisted. "If one of the creatures did come out of deep water, we'd be able to see it in plenty of time and hit the shore."

Loch thought that over a moment and decided it really wasn't a bad idea. "I'll tell you what," Loch said. "First, I'll ride up to the grid by myself. If it looks really safe, I'll come back and get you."

"No way," Zaidee said. "If you left me here, maybe one of those creatures would come out of the water and eat me in the trailer."

"Plesiosaurs don't go on land."

"Well, then, I might take a nap and sleep-walk into the lake—"

"Let's just forget the whole thing," Loch said, ticked off. He changed from a spinner to a popper, tossing it far out. He made a half dozen more casts. There wasn't a decent fish in sight, and it was a really beautiful day. The deep water was plenty far from shore. There really wasn't any way anything could strike out at them without their seeing it coming. He made a few more casts with Zaidee just tapping her foot, watching him.

"All right." He broke down. "Let's skip the fishing. We can at least take a boat ride in the shallows."

They both laughed, and raced up to the trailer to grab gear for the boat.

"You pack pretzels and sandwiches," Loch said. "I'll ice the cooler."

Zaidee threw the refrigerator door open,

pulled out some roast beef, ham, and cheese, tossed them onto white bread, and put them in the picnic basket. She left the pretzels in case Dr. Sam wanted some with a beer when he got home that night. Besides, she liked the Wheat Thins and Mallomars better.

"I'll wait for you in the boat," she called to Loch. She grabbed the picnic basket in one hand, the laptop in the other, and went out the door.

"Be right down," Loch yelled.

Zaidee was sitting in the bow seat and was on the second screen of Crashers by the time Loch boarded with the cooler and scuba gear.

Zaidee's jaw dropped. "Are you out of your mind?"

"I probably won't use it," Loch said, slapping the air tank. "But maybe I'll want to get a closer look at something."

"That's not the problem. Something might want to get a closer look at you!"

"Lighten up," Loch said, starting the motor on the first pull. He threw it into forward gear, and the churning propeller thrust them quickly away from the dock. He turned long before the deep water, brought the boat in close to shore, and held it steady. The sky was clear. Even the deepest water of the lake had given way to an intense, spectacular blue.

There were more logs in the water than usual. Loch knew they must have drifted over from the north side of the lake after the storm had swollen the log pond at the old mill. He kept his head high as the boat rushed across the water. One thing he knew they didn't need was to hit a log and bend the prop.

Loch had always thrilled to moving fast across a lake on a perfect day. On the brink of the open water, his mind would flood with thoughts, so many at the same time that he felt part of a vast kaleidoscope. He would think of poems and music. Sometimes he'd just remember his mother and what it had been like when they were all a family. Lately, during the last few months, he had begun to think most about feeling lonely, and what he was going to do with his life. All the problems and questions lurking in his mind and heart would tumble toward answers in the hugeness of a lake.

The outboard churned out a good-sized wake, a trail of bubbles and waves fanning out and violating the calmness of the water for a great distance behind them. He guided the boat along, taking note of half-sunken trees and patches of lake grass that he knew might hold big fish. There were stretches of tall pines that threw their branches out over the water to make the great cooling shadows largemouth bass liked on hot afternoons. He glimpsed sudden, whirling circles where the sound of the outboard interrupted pickerel basking in the sun. Over all were the mountains rimming the lake, looming tall like protective, watchful giants.

Zaidee went on high alert when Loch cut the speed and shifted into neutral near the salmon grid. He put on his scuba mask and hung his head over the side of the boat as it drifted toward shore.

"What are you looking for, *fingers*?" Zaidee asked.

Loch put his hands in the water and began paddling. Slowly, easily, he guided the flat-bottomed boat in closer to the shore where the first beast had been trapped and broken through the net. In the clear shallows he could see the scrapings on the bottom of the lake where the creature had struggled. There were fragments from the ripped rope net wedged between small rocks, shreds waving, pointing toward the shore as though there were some sort of undertow.

Loch lifted his head out of the water to get his bearings on the salmon grid. Its great aluminum-and-steel structures were a hundred yards farther along the shore.

"I want to wait on land," Zaidee said.

"That's a good idea," Loch said. He got the boat into a position off a weed bed and goosed the throttle. The boat hurtled forward, lifting its bow and nuzzling up onto the shore. Zaidee jumped off and secured the anchor line around a tree.

"Want to eat now?" she asked.

"Later," Loch said. He wanted to check out the scrapings close up.

"Okay. You lug the cooler."

She grabbed the picnic basket and laptop and made her way to a large, flat rock over-looking the grid and inlet. She started to play Crashers as her brother set the cooler down and began to put on his scuba gear.

"Hey," Zaidee said, "I'm getting interference on the screen again."

"Two thick black lines?"

"Just one thin one, right through the middle."

"Maybe it's that," Loch said, pointing to what looked like a cement bunker at the near side of the grid.

"Crashers was working fine until we got here."

"There's probably a lot of electrical stuff around."

Zaidee watched her brother walking like a frog in his big fins. "Loch, if you hear me scream, it means there's something you don't want to meet heading your way."

"Gotcha!"

Loch spit in his mask to defog it and did a final check on the oxygen flow from his air tank. He put on a weight belt, then backed slowly into the water. When he was waist deep, he let himself fall backward and went under.

The water was cold and crystal clear near the shore. With a single kick of his flippers he launched himself forward toward the scrapings on the gravel bottom. Loch had long ago worked out an underwater swimming stroke he'd never seen other divers use. He'd thrust out both arms together, then cup his palms and pull them back like a two-handed racket return in tennis. He'd combine each stroke with a single kick of his long, powerful legs. He knew it was unorthodox, but it gave him the speed and endurance he wanted—so much so, he had grown to feel as much at home underwater as on land.

The main disturbance of bottom stones began about forty feet from the shore. Loch glided over the markings, keeping one eye on the dark wall of peat water that lay a hundred feet farther out. Even some of the larger stones had been upset by the thrashing of the beast's body, but at the same spot he noticed something he hadn't seen when he had peered down from the bass boat. There was a *second* set of scrapings near the first set, less deep, less violent. They led at an angle toward the shore. More shreds of rope net lined these scrapings, in motion like small, brown eels being washed by a current.

Loch propelled himself along the path of the second markings. At first he thought that they might be from the beast's immense neck, that in its struggle to escape it had dragged its neck along the bottom. But the scuffs were too long and too far for that. The thought that they might have been caused by another smaller creature crossed his mind as he felt the pull of the current. At first it was a gentle force from behind him, water pushing him toward the shore. He looked ahead to see a darkness beneath a large rock ledge. By the time he was close enough to see it was the entrance to a narrow cave, it was too late. He was caught in the undertow. He tried to fight its pull, turned to throw his cupped hands against the current and kick with his full power. Still, he lost ground. The current grew stronger, banged his air tank against the bottom stones, rushed him faster, rougher.

He grabbed out for a rock, but the flux pulled at his legs. His weight belt scraped at his stomach, and the rock rolled loose. Finally, he lost complete control and was swept into the narrow dark hole.

He couldn't see as his body was whirled and tumbled, the air tank banging against the unseen sides. Faster he went, the water picking up speed until he was on a rough, dangerous water slide, dropping at a very great angle. He fought to keep his mask on, to maintain his bite on the breathing tube while using his arms to protect his head.

It seemed to him he had traveled the length of a football field beneath the earth before he glimpsed light again. The tunnel was larger now, and the relentless banging against the rock sides all but stopped. When he lifted his head above the surface of the rushing water he realized he was moving through a cavern. Sunlight shot down from a hole in the side of a natural crystal dome, a structure the likes of which he'd seen only once before, when his father had taken him and Zaidee on a hunt for minerals in New Mexico.

"Hey!" He tried calling as he was swept along the sheer edges of the underground river.

His shouts were greeted by shrieks from a swarm of bats spiraling upward toward the top of the dome. He was swept out of the chamber, and then into another blackness, the water falling faster still. In the next lighted chamber he glimpsed the earth above and saw that it had eroded. What was left of the cave's ceiling was lined with glistening red-and-white stalactites. Exposed tree roots climbed down the sides like thick, curling serpents. Then the water flowed

out of the cavern and into a less exotic landscape, that of the Vermont mountainsides. Now
Loch relaxed, believing he would survive. The
waterway was narrow but as fast, strong, and
deep as a trout stream.

He heard a low, chilling noise as he struggled to reach the reeds and shore bushes. It was
a roaring he had heard on other expeditions. He
grabbed at a birch root protruding from the
steep bank, spit out his mouthpiece, and un-
hooked the tank and weight belt. But the root
gave way. He saw the brink coming, saw the
great height. Quickly, he was washed over the
edge and began to plummet down.

He had fallen too long and too far to keep
his eyes open. He felt the crash into the pool
below and the crush of bubbles as if he had
been thrust beneath the surface of a violent
Jacuzzi. He held his breath for a very, very long
time. Then, as if he had been wiped out by an
ocean wave, the tumult subsided. His head
bobbed to the surface, and he found himself in
a shimmering, clear pool beneath the waterfall.

THE CALLING

Loch swam to the edge of the pool, exhausted. He managed to drag himself up onto a large slab of granite and tug off his fins. He had swallowed a lot of water, and it took him a while to catch his breath. He knew Zaidee would be looking for him.

He stood to get his bearings. When he looked up at the top of the waterfall, he saw a familiar ridge and the back of the cement bunker.

"Hey!" he yelled. "Hey, Zaidee!"

He called twice more before Zaidee could tell where his voice was coming from. When she realized he had disappeared, she had checked the shoreline. She wasn't expecting to hear his voice calling from behind her.

Zaidee climbed the knoll to the grid control bunker. From there she could see Loch standing far down the slope.

"What are you doing there?" she shouted, glad to see his grinning face. The one thing she always knew was that Loch was able to take care of himself.

He waved. "Come on down!"

"All right, all right!"

She scooped up the picnic basket and laptop, made her way down the steep path along the stream, then cut in toward the pool. When she got closer, she saw that Loch was flushed and minus the scuba gear.

"Did you fall down that?" she asked, eyeing the waterfall.

"And then some," he said. "I think something else might have come down it too." He described the set of smaller scrapings.

"Maybe they're from a beaver or an otter."

"Maybe."

"I don't know about you, but I'm hungry." Zaidee sat down on the rock and opened the picnic basket. "Do you want roast beef or ham and cheese?"

"Not now," Loch said, staring down into the pool. He saw his mask and air tank dead center on the bottom, and slipped on his fins again.

"You're not going back in, are you?"

SPLASH.

"You're crazy," Zaidee called after him.

Loch retrieved his mask on the first dive. Next, he brought up the air tank. He knew he'd probably never see the weight belt again, but that didn't matter. Quickly, he got the scuba gear back on and dropped back into the pool, this time leaving a gurgling stream of air bubbles behind him. Across from the deep, gravelly center was the wall of boiling chaos where the waterfall crashed into the pool. On both sides were thick clusters of lush water plants and floating lilies with enormous stems and roots reaching down like tentacles to anchor among the rocks.

Loch settled on the bottom. Slowly, he moved on toward the underwater garden. He veered away from the bedlam of the falls, sliding into the light and shadows of the eerie waterscape.

It was here that he first heard the music. At least, that's what it sounded like to him—a single muted instrument being played, a kind of otherworldly singing. It was faint and plaintive, like strains from a distant cello.

Suddenly, there was a fast, quick movement in the thick of the water plants, and Loch knew he was not alone at the bottom of the pool. He swam closer, very slowly, but his mask began to fog. He would have to fix it immediately. He stopped, braced his feet on the bottom stones, and pushed for the surface. His head popped out of the water next to the slab of granite.

"You see anything?" Zaidee asked, busy eating her sandwich and playing Crashers.

Loch pulled his mask off. "I'm not sure." There was no point in telling Zaidee anything until he had checked it out.

"You know, the screen's even worse now," Zaidee complained. "The squiggly line's going ballistic. You want half a roast-beef sandwich?"

"No thanks." Loch spit into his mask again

and smudged the saliva around on the plastic with his fingers.

"Hey." Zaidee gagged. "I'm eating!"

Loch put the mask back on, kicked his legs high into the air, and dove back to the bottom of the pool.

Again he heard the faint, curious music. He knew it wasn't caused by any water in his ears, and he certainly hadn't been down long or deep enough to have delirium levels of nitrogen in his blood. Once more he approached the water plants. This time he glimpsed the dark blur rushing behind a rock, a creature about the size of a seal. He knew even seals bite if their territory is invaded, so he used his fins to glide slowly up and over the top of the rock. The cello sound changed suddenly into an ominous hum.

When he looked down, all he could think was, Oh my God.

Directly beneath him was the black, bony, plated back of what had to be a very young plesiosaur. Adrenaline shot into Loch's blood. The long neck of the creature lifted, then twisted so its head could turn and look up at him. Loch stared into the face of the creature, a miniature of the ghastly, terrifying Rogue.

Hummmmm . . .

The hum became more of a growl. He realized the creature's mouth could open at any moment, and the little beast might lunge for his throat. Loch let his legs settle slowly, until his fins lay on the top of the rock. The creature's eyes stayed riveted on him, but its frightening humming dropped a pitch, becoming softer and less threatening. Loch saw bruises on the creature's ribbed fins and body. He knew it had to have been cornered with its mother at the nets, then washed through the cavern and over the falls. Now it was trapped in the pool, hurt and dazed. Loch had seen the same sad look in the eyes of a coyote he once saw limping out of a canyon after a fire. The flames had burned the coyote's back, compromising its wild instincts.

The humming stopped.

Loch moved and settled slowly to one side of the rock. Now the creature was in front of him.

"Okay, fellah . . . it's okay." Loch spoke softly through the mouthpiece. He knew to minimize the stream of bubbles from his air tank and let his words reverberate deeply from his chest, a type of intoning his father had taught him when they had hand-fed groupers and sea turtles off tropical reefs.

The creature raised its bumpy snout.

"Good boy . . . uh, good little boy," Loch repeated as he reached out his right hand just a few inches, as he would to pet a strange dog. "Nice little plesiosaur . . ."

Suddenly the hoods above the creature's eyes lifted, revealing the full size of its enormous eyes. It reared up, drew its head back, then shot it forward, brandishing a massive mouth of jagged teeth. Like a demonic swan, it lunged its snout again and again at Loch, never touching him, but causing him to fall over backward. Loch froze with the creature on top of him, its teeth whirling just above his face. Loch's heart beat crazily, until the lunges stopped. Finally the creature closed its mouth, slowly retreating from Loch's head. Lock took a deep breath.

It doesn't want to hurt me, Loch told himself, astounded.

Inch by inch, Loch eased himself away from

the creature and righted himself. It began to make a new sound. At first it was a type of clicking, as if it were sending out a kind of sonar to examine Loch. But the clicking sounds changed into the eerily beautiful music again.

"You make music when you feel safe," Loch said to the creature. "Music when you trust someone . . ."

Loch didn't know the words to express the thrill of being in the presence of the creature, but he knew he was witnessing something rare and precious and inexplicable.

Loch pushed against the bottom and swam slowly upward. He surfaced near Zaidee and spit out his mouthpiece.

"Give me a sandwich!" he gasped, deciding not to tell her yet about the creature.

"Say please," Zaidee insisted.

"Please."

"Roast beef or ham?" she asked, offering both.

He grabbed the roast-beef sandwich, bit down on the mouthpiece, and quickly dove back beneath the surface.

"Hey!" Zaidee yelled, watching the sandwich go under.

Loch reached bottom. The creature hadn't moved. Again it started its music. Slowly, he held out the disintegrating sandwich, letting the bread and meat float down in front of the creature. Quickly, its head reared back, then snapped forward, over and over again until every speck of the sandwich was devoured.

"Good boy . . . you're a little hungry . . . good fellah." Loch knew there had to be small fish in the pool—shoreline crappies and sunfish from the lake that had gotten caught up in the underwater current the same way he had—but hardly enough for a growing young plesiosaur. Loch attempted to imitate the sounds, the pitch, and the rhythm, of the creature's music. Eventually, he inched his hand out toward its head. The creature allowed him to slide his fingers gently over the knobby plating on the skull.

"You need a name," Loch told the creature, as he continued to pet its head. He thought about calling it Dan or Steve, but a human name didn't seem to fit. He remembered they had named its mother Beast. "Son of Beast" also didn't sound right.

Loch stopped petting the creature for a moment and moved his hands to adjust his mask.

The creature seemed disappointed. It lifted its head until Loch's hand was touching it. Again Loch petted it, then tried moving his hand away. Once more the creature slid its head under Loch's hand.

Loch laughed. "You want more."

Finally Loch tried moving away a few feet. The creature moved with him. "You're smart," Loch told the creature. "And you probably want another sandwich. I'll be right back, okay?"

Loch started to swim, reaching his cupped hands out, pulling at the water. When Loch looked back, he saw the creature swimming after him, its fins thrusting it forward smoothly, powerfully.

"How about this?" Loch said, bubbles rising as he looped over backward. The creature stayed with him, circling at his side. By now Loch knew the creature understood it was a game, and they began to spin and turn joyously beneath the water.

➤

Zaidee knew Loch's air supply would be running out soon, that he'd have to come up. She hung over the edge of the pool, watching Loch cavort in and out of the deep shadows with something that looked to her like a big otter. It appeared they were playing a weird game of tag.

When Loch finally started up toward her, the creature followed almost to the surface, but then disappeared into the water plants.

Loch's head bobbed up near the ledge.

"What is that thing down there?" Zaidee asked. "Whatever it is, I think it's making the static line on Crashers go bonkers."

Loch pulled himself out. "You've got to see it to believe it," he gasped. "You got another sandwich?"

"There's half a ham and cheese left."

"Hold it over the edge," Loch told her. "It needs to know you're a friend."

Zaidee scrunched up her face. "I am not that thing's friend!"

"Come on," Loch said. "Don't you want to see it?" He took the sandwich and stuck it in Zaidee's hand. "Just let it watch you putting it in the water. It can see what you're doing."

"Big deal. Dad let me feed otters in the Galápagos when I was three years old."

"Do it!"

He helped hold Zaidee as she reached out and set the sandwich in the water. She no sooner let go of it than the head of the creature exploded from the surface, hurtling the bread and meat into the air. As the food fell down, all Zaidee could see and hear was a whirling blur of ferocious, gnashing teeth. Zaidee screamed until the creature had finished its feeding, closed its mouth, and settled quietly at the edge of the pond to look at them.

"Nasty," Zaidee said.

"Right," Loch agreed. "It's ugly as sin, but it's all ours!"

INVASION

It didn't take Zaidee long to see past the gnashing teeth, beyond the horror of the creature's face, to realize what a mind-boggling, cool thing they had found. She fed it every last piece of food they had, including the Mallomars.

"It loves chocolate," Zaidee said. "It's really smart."

Loch laughed. "I think it would rather snack on a nice, fat salmon." Then, deadly serious, he continued, "You can't tell anyone about this."

"What about Dad?" Zaidee asked.

"Of course we're going to have to tell him," Loch said. "But if Cavenger finds out, how long do you think it'd be before he'd have his name on a plaque with the creature stuffed and under glass in the British Museum?"

➤

Loch and Zaidee swam and played with the beast all afternoon, but finally the time came when they had to leave.

"We have to go now," Loch told the creature. It was as if the moment the thought had entered Loch's mind, the creature understood. It began to make rapid, sad sounds.

CLICK CLICK . . .

CLACK CLICK CLACK . . .

"What's it doing?" Loch wondered.

"It doesn't want us to go," Zaidee said.

The creature lifted the hoods of its eyes high and stared at Loch and Zaidee.

CLICK CLACK . . . CLICK . . .

"It knows we're going to leave it alone again," Zaidee said, giving the creature a last gentle pat on its head.

"We'll be back," Loch promised.

The creature swam back and forth in the pool, lifting its head high to watch Loch and Zaidee until they disappeared over the ridge. By the time they had made it back to the boat,

Loch had thought of a name for the creature. "Remember that Robert Burns poem 'To a Mouse'?" Loch asked Zaidee. "I had to memorize it once."

"I don't remember."

"It was about a mouse who ends up homeless because its nest gets dug up by a farmer's plow," Loch said, as he got into the boat and primed the motor. "I remember only the first line, 'Wee, sleekit, cow'rin', tim'rous beastie . . .'"

Zaidee untied the anchor rope, pushed the boat off, and settled back into the bow seat. "That's a long name."

"Wee Beastie," Loch said, leaning over the outboard and pulling the start cord. "That's his name."

"Wee Beastie?"

"What do you think?"

Zaidee turned the name over in her mind as the motor coughed to life. "I think I like it," she said.

"Then it's settled." Loch threw the boat into gear and gave it full throttle. The boat hurtled back out onto the lake. The tall pines along the north shore cast huge shadows across the shallows, making the drift logs harder to see.

"Dad will freak when he finds out we took the boat," Zaidee said, worried.

"Not when we show him Wee Beastie," Loch said.

Zaidee opened the laptop and brought Crashers up on the screen. "The game picked up the sounds from yesterday's creatures too," Zaidee said. "How come their lines were on this before they showed on the sonar screens?"

"Look, it's a computer," Loch reminded her. "Maybe there's something about having Crashers with 580 megabytes that turns it into a kind of receiver for sonar."

"What's a megabyte?" Zaidee wanted to know. "You said one day you'd teach me all about computers."

"It's going to take more than one day, but what I'm saying is maybe the creatures register on our screen because of those sounds they make, like whales and dolphins do. Maybe Wee Beastie and these guys make more concentrated and directed sounds, waves that can travel through water, then vibrate the surface and continue through the air. Who knows?"

"There are no interference lines now,"

Zaidee said, keeping one eye on the edge of the deep water.

When they got back, they tied the boat at the dock and hurried up to the trailer. They tossed their gear inside and walked down the driveway to the south road to look for a lift to the base. A beat-up Toyota 4x4 headed their way. Loch waved it down. It was only after the truck stopped that they both realized it was Jesse Sanderson, the caretaker of the logging mill, behind the wheel.

"I'm not riding with him," Zaidee whispered as Loch opened the door. "He's probably drunk as usual."

"Where you kids headin'?" Jesse asked, his mouth open wide, proudly revealing his gold front teeth.

Loch decided he'd get Jesse to say a few more words to see if he had been doing any afternoon nipping. "Hi, Mr. Sanderson. We were out to see you at the logging mill with our father, remember?"

Jesse took a closer look at them as he lifted his rifle off the front seat and stuck it on the shelf below the rear window. "Oh, yeah," he said, his big belly hitting into the steering wheel.

"Wanted to know what I'd seen in the lake . . . and I told you. Something with a head big as a barrel, yes, sir, big as a barrel . . . "

"He's sober," Loch mouthed to Zaidee as he slid into the middle seat. "Can we ride along as far as the base?" Loch asked Jesse.

"Glad for the company," he said.

Zaidee made a face. She hopped up next to her brother and slammed the door. Jesse put the truck into gear. Its front end had a major shimmy, but Jesse was driving slowly enough.

"Seen anything in the lake lately?" Loch asked, checking to see how much Jesse knew. Everyone at camp knew he was a big creep, and he was always wandering around trying to stick his big red nose into the expedition's business.

"Can't say I have," Jesse said.

"What are you doing on this side of the lake?" Zaidee wanted to know.

"Ran out of supplies. Had a little shopping to do."

Zaidee turned to look behind her. She saw a half dozen cases of beer jiggling in the bed of the truck.

At the main gate of the base, Jesse was surprised to see the encampment swarming with new recruits and heavy equipment. The loud, steady clanking of a pneumatic driver cut through the air as a crew of sweating men completed the installation of a high link fence topped with barbed wire.

"What's going on around here?" Jesse asked the guard. "Looks like you're goin' to war."

The guard put on a phony, folksy smile. "Nothing much. Just getting ready for another sweep tomorrow."

"No kidding," Jesse said like he cared. The only thing that really interested him was a pile of lumber and a couple of big toolboxes. He figured he'd go home, have a couple of drinks, then come back and see what he could rip off.

Loch and Zaidee thanked Jesse for the lift, jumped down from the truck, and ran in through the gate. Construction workers were throwing up additional structures and setting up machinery. A large military helicopter made a pass along the shoreline, then stirred up a big cloud of dust as it landed on a freshly leveled pad.

They spotted John Randolph cutting across the base in a jeep. "Have you seen Dr. Sam?" Loch called.

"Hc's on *The Revelation*," Randolph shouted back.

Loch and Zaidee walked toward the dock. The old brown fishing trawlers were backed up to the shore with their crews feeding shiny metal netting from two flatbed trucks onto the boats' huge, rusted spindles. To the left of the Sea-B several dozen men were helping guide a large, sleek boat into the water to join the fleet of skiffs.

"What kind of boat is that?" Zaidee wanted to know.

"Looks like a converted PT boat," Loch said. He remembered seeing them in World War II footage on TV and knew they were famous for their speed; some were some still used by the Coast Guard for running down harbor drug traffic.

When they reached the dock, supplies were being unloaded from trucks onto the water taxis. Zaidee held Loch's hand as he guided them through the horde and up the gangplank onto the yacht.

They found Dr. Sam in the control room with Cavenger, Emilio, and several other electronics technicians.

"Dad," Loch called from the doorway.

Dr. Sam looked up from calibrating the graphic recorders. He was surprised to see Loch and Zaidee.

Cavenger saw them too. "Get rid of them," he ordered Dr. Sam.

Dr. Sam moved quickly to the door, his face flushed. "What are you doing here? I told you the base was off-limits today."

"We've got something to tell you—" Zaidee started.

"Not now," Dr. Sam cut her off, sharply.

"It's important, Dad," Loch said.

"I told you to stay at the trailer." Dr. Sam raised his voice, wanting Cavenger to know it wasn't his fault the kids had shown up. Loch picked up on exactly what his father was doing. He really hated it whenever his dad was afraid to stand up to Cavenger even when it just meant taking a minute out to talk to his own kids.

"Daddy, something wonderful—" Zaidee tried to get the words out.

"Look. Just leave. And I mean on the double," Dr. Sam yelled at them, acting like a stranger as he practically pushed them out the door.

Zaidee stared down at the deck. She wanted to cry. They had the most wonderful news in the world to tell their father, and he wouldn't even give them a minute.

Loch put his arm around his sister. "Sorry we bothered you," he told Dr. Sam.

"It's just not the right time," Dr. Sam said, guilt crawling into his voice now. "You're going to get me fired." He went back into the control room and slammed the door.

"He doesn't mean it," Loch told Zaidee.

"Yes he does," Zaidee said.

Loch kept his arm around Zaidee as they walked along the deck. "What do you say we go down to Sarah's cabin?"

Zaidee ducked out from under his arm and glared at him. "No thanks. She's probably having a bad hair day. You're not going to tell *her* about Wee Beastie, are you?"

"No," Loch said. "Let's just see how she's feeling."

"That's a definite pass."

"You used to like her," Loch reminded

Zaidee. "I don't get it. Lately, all you do is put her down."

"Because she's turned into a really horrible, spoiled, rich brat, that's why," Zaidee said.

"How can you say that?"

"It's easy. Her father gives her everything she wants, and she's got too many Harrods and trendy store shopping bags."

"What does it matter how many shopping bags she has?"

"She always has them on display in her room, with all the brand names and logos of her clothes staring at us. Remember last year I had this nice new blouse from Penney's and it had a little fox logo on it, and she saw it and kept asking, 'Who has the fox, oh, who has the fox?' Remember that? Her father lets her buy so much junk, nothing means anything to her, including people."

Loch flicked his hand up the back of Zaidee's neck. "Zaidee, don't be jealous."

"Look, just don't tell her about Wee Beastie is all I'm saying," Zaidee pleaded. "He's ours."

"Okay," Loch said.

"Promise?"

"I promise."

"Excellent," Zaidee said. "In that case, I'll wait on the rear deck. I'll be lounging."

Loch went down the stairway to the lower deck. What he really needed was a minute to himself to shake off the way his father had treated them. He knew the whole power play around Cavenger was very complicated, but the bottom line was that his father jumped whenever Cavenger blew his whistle. It seemed to be eating away part of his father's very being.

➤

The second cabin on the left was Sarah's. Loch combed his hair with his fingers and knocked on the door.

"What?" came Sarah's voice.

"It's me," Loch said.

The door opened. Sarah stood there, looking sleepy in pajamas. "Loch, what's the matter?" she asked, when she saw how flushed he looked. She had come to know the look, and knew what caused it.

"Nothing."

"What are you doing here?"

"Zaidee and I stopped down to see Dad," Loch explained. "She's up on the sundeck. How's it going?"

Sarah brushed her hair back from her face. "All that riveting and hammering going on around here is driving me crazy," she said. She closed the door behind them. "I really needed sack time. I had a hundred and forty-three nightmares about that horrendous monster trying to kebab me!"

"Yesterday *was* a nightmare" was all Loch said, knowing he couldn't tell her about Wee Beastie. "Looks like your father's still going to try to catch one of the creatures."

"That's all he talks about every second," Sarah admitted. "I think he's starting to go a little psycho. He knows if he gets one, it'll be his vindication against all the people who have said he was nuts for going on crazy expeditions all his life. Let's take a walk."

"Okay."

"I just have to throw on some clothes."

"I'll wait outside."

"You can just turn around."

Loch turned his back, shifting awkwardly from foot to foot while she threw off her pjs and put on a top and jeans.

"Do you remember how you used to drive me crazy pretending to eat out of dog-food

cans?" she asked. "And you'd lift the cheese off
a pizza and wear it on your face?"

"How do you know it wasn't Mighty Dog?"

Sarah laughed as she slipped on multicol-
ored leather boots. "I guess we both always
liked weird things." She led the way out into
the hall and up to the sundeck. Zaidee was
stretched out on a chaise longue reading a magazine. She made a face when she saw Loch had
brought Sarah.

"Hi, Zaidee," Sarah said.

"Hello," Zaidee said. She grimaced at the
sight of Sarah's boots and went back to reading
her magazine. Sarah and Loch went to the railing and looked down at the dock below to
watch all the activity.

"Say, do you think you can borrow some
wheels tomorrow?" Loch asked.

"Sure. Dad always lets me take one of the
jeeps. What's up?"

"I need to get a few things from town."

An armored vehicle pulled up to the edge of
the dock. The driver got out, unlocked the rear
doors, and threw them open to reveal a few
racks of high-caliber rifles. Randolph was on
hand with a clipboard, assigning the guns and

ammunition to the fleet crews. Sarah started walking to the bow. "Why all the artillery?" Loch asked, following her as the riveting started in again, vibrating through the entire yacht. "Nobody would want to kill a plesiosaur. They'd want to study them. It's the chance of a lifetime."

"Tell that to Erdon," Sarah said.

Loch stopped at the railing. He stared down at the construction in progress at the front of *The Revelation.* A welder in a protective mask held a blowtorch, sealing a seam on a metal base. The riveters worked securing an immense steel harpoon gun to the deck. Nearby, its lethal ammunition lay in a heap—monstrous steel arrows to harvest a leviathan.

"Dad told me he doesn't need to take a creature alive," Sarah said. "He says even a fin or a tail, any piece of one of them, would prove they exist."

THE LOGGING MILL

Jesse Sanderson stood up, went to the refrigerator in the kitchen of his cozy apartment above the boathouse, and took out another beer. He had just finished watching the last of three laser discs on his new Sony entertainment system. The realism of the bullet sounds and throbbing music made the ruddy-faced old-timer marvel at the advances of technology.

From the picture window in the living room he could see the sunset and the first fingers of night fog crawling in from the water. It was on a night like this that he had sighted the creature far out in the lake, the creature with "a head the size of a big barrel," as he liked to tell the story at the local bars. The night of the sighting he'd had a great deal more to drink than usual, but he was certain he had seen it anyway and swore by it. Whether it was really some appalling prehistoric creature of the lake or a swimming moose did not matter to him at all. The only thing that concerned him was that nothing happen around Lake Alban that would make him lose his job and comfortable apartment.

Jesse's employment as caretaker of the logging mill earned him twenty-eight thousand dollars a year, enough to keep him in good beer and gold teeth, he always joked. His job, paradoxically, was to make sure work was not done. In the age of political correctness and environmental awareness, the owner of the mill was being given a lot of money every year to ensure the propagation of certain fish and eels by keeping the logging mill closed. The salmon grid was one of the governor's little babies, and as long as the mill was kept in working order, but not used, the government would continue to pay.

Jesse liked living alone. He had grown up on his own. He hated pets. It probably went back to his childhood, when he had been bitten by a stray Doberman and had had to have two weeks of rabies shots. His dislike of animals had made him a good trapper and put a few extra dollars in his pocket every month. The log pond and feeder stream were alive with beavers. He would set several traps at once, close to each other, so when one animal got caught, another would try to eat it and get caught, and so on. Whenever he made the rounds of the local taverns, he enjoyed telling everybody the only really good pet he had was his shotgun.

He opened the beer, his sixth since late afternoon, took his dinner out of the microwave, and went back to his favorite chair in front of the picture window. He put on the television to watch the evening news when he heard the sounds again. He had long ago learned to discount the regular noises from below, the slap of waves or the knock of the outboard and canoe hitting the cushion tires of the boathouse slips.

The sounds this evening were the same, but louder than those he'd heard over the last few weeks—more like a kind of singing.

Kids with a radio was what he had thought it was on the other nights, and it drove him crazy. Tonight the sounds were louder, closer, and he felt it was definitely kids who were trespassing and were going to make his dinner get cold.

Jesse had seen his share of town kids using the mill road as a lovers' lane. Why was it that people, especially young people, had to be so damn annoying! Jesse looked out the side windows. He didn't see any cars parked or campfires. He took his shotgun, checked to make sure it was loaded, and started down the boathouse stairs.

The fog rushed at him as he checked the motorboat and canoe tied up in the double slip of the boathouse. Once he had caught a couple of kids rowing from the lake into the slips. They got as far as untying the canoe before they were looking down the barrel of his gun. He had to laugh remembering the look on their faces. They knew it wouldn't have bothered him very much to have pulled that trigger, but that night he gave the boys a break.

Jesse took a few deep breaths of the moist, crisp air. He could really feel the beers now. The only thing he could smell was the thick scent of pine and sweet bass. The singing seemed to come from the pier. He opened the door of the boathouse and started out toward the sounds.

BAM.

He fired his shotgun into the air. "You lousy kids and your radios keep out of here!" he brayed out at the lake. "I can see your boat!" he lied. "I'm coming out there and I'm gonna blast it!"

Jesse reloaded his gun. A single shot usually got any kids to take off, but there were still sounds. Now that he was out on the pier, the sounds changed. They became something different. Now they were some sort of low hum he had never heard before. It was a little confusing at first, what with the racket of the crickets in the bulrushes and cicadas in the trees.

He stopped, took a good listen. He decided whatever it was, it wasn't human—maybe some kind of water insect or small mammal. That made him relax. One thing he didn't need tonight after those beers was a lot of legal paperwork and hassle for blowing some trespassing kid's head off.

He pulled back both hammers on the gun and moved farther along on the pier. The weather-beaten boards had grown creaky and slippery with age. A wall of fog marched on him, cutting his visibility down to about twenty feet. The humming was growing louder now. He heard a large bass jump about sixty yards to the left, making a loud splash. When he glimpsed the end of the pier, the humming suddenly stopped. There was some kind of movement in the water below. Whatever the thing was, it had gone under. He looked over the sides of the pier but saw nothing.

"Hello out here," he said to the fog, as he knelt down on one knee, his shotgun ready. "Hey, little hummers, where are you?"

The humming sounds started again. This time they sounded like they were coming from right under him.

"Nice, little hummers, let me see you," he said. He got down on his hands and knees, slid his feet back, and lay on his stomach. He one-handed the gun now, as he peered over the edge and inched his head out over the water. The humming stopped. He looked back under the pier, ready to thrust the shotgun forward and fire beneath him. There were only the shadows of mold and algae growing up the sides of the pilings. Instinct told him to lift his head and check behind him, but there was nothing. He stayed lying flat on his stomach until the humming began again. Now he was certain the sound came from the water directly off the front of the pier.

"Where are you?" he asked. "You're like some kind of garfish, shy of the hook, some kind of bullfrog. Maybe a turtle?" Jesse started to laugh at himself as he lifted his gun into position. "Come on, let's see you guys so I can give you a nice, little surprise. . . . "

Jesse felt a breeze. The fog bank split open to reveal a pair of eyes set behind a snout. To Jesse, it looked like the head of a small alligator, some kind of reptile not much longer than six or seven feet. He knew the size of alligators pretty well because when he was younger he had spent some time hunting them in Florida.

At the time, six feet was the minimum legal size for harvesting and skinning a gator.

"There you are, nice, little, ugly fellah," Jesse crooned. The creature was small, whatever it was, and Jesse wanted to nail it with a single shot. He kept talking to it, letting it hum and hum, as he sat up and swung his legs around and out over the pier. He raised his left hand to support the shotgun, as the index finger of his right hand crawled around the trigger. The distance was comfortable. In a moment it would have been over, but the fog closed again. Damn! He would have to wait for the next breeze.

The humming continued, and Jesse started humming along with it, his eyes glued down the double barrels. After a few minutes another breeze came, slowly pushing away the fog until he could see a good thirty feet beyond the end of the dock. The gator head was gone. The humming was coming from both sides of him now. He turned to look to the left when suddenly a head on a long, black, shiny neck snapped forward from the right. It sank its teeth into Jesse's right foot. The motion and the pain cut through the alcohol in his brain, making him turn his head to the right, but a second head and neck lurched in from the left, its mouth and teeth locking onto his other foot.

Jesse cried out in pain and surprise, his shotgun firing uselessly into the air. Instinctively, he kicked his legs, attempting to throw the creatures off. When they finally dropped away, he drew his legs up to his body, reaching down to stop the terrible hurt. He stared in disbelief when he saw the dark and staining rush of blood on the wooden planks. Both of his feet were missing, severed at the ankles.

Screaming, Jesse threw his body backward, away from the edge of the pier. He tried to stand on his stumps but crashed forward. He started to pull his body back down the pier, leaving a thick trail of blood behind him. His thoughts were insane now. He told himself that if he could only make it back to the boathouse, back up the stairs to his favorite chair and waiting dinner, then he would be safe. He would wake up to find it all was a very bad dream.

Unfortunately for Jesse, the pair of long-necked heads again rose from the lake and lunged back over the edge of the pier. The creatures bit at his bloody stumps, their mouths snapping forward again and again. He struck at them with the butt of the shotgun, cracked them on their bony, plated skulls. For a few delirious moments, he even thought he was winning.

Then he heard a louder humming, one that shook his body and the planking beneath. A massive head lifted above the pier like a dark and terrible moon. Immediately, the two smaller creatures scurried off, and as Jesse looked into the massive yellow eyes of the Rogue, he profoundly understood that his life was over.

THE GRID

"Thanks for saving me some dinner," Dr. Sam said, sliding into the dining nook of the trailer. Loch and Zaidee had long before made a big bowl of spaghetti and meatballs and set a plate aside for their father. He forced a chuckle, hoping they would make his apology easy for him. "What was so important with you guys this afternoon?"

They could tell he was feeling guilty about the way he had treated them on *The Revelation*, but they were past feeling hurt now. All they were interested in was whether or not they should tell him about Wee Beastie.

"Nothing was important," Zaidee said, pouring herself a glass of milk and sitting as far away from her father as possible.

"It had to be something," Dr. Sam pursued. "I'm sorry I was so short, but I was under a lot of pressure from Cavenger." He knew he wasn't as good a parent as his wife had been. Their mother had had endless patience and the ability to drop everything she was doing and listen to their small problems.

"Do you always have to do everything Cavenger says?" Loch asked, sliding into the seat across from his father.

"Son, we've been over this before." Dr. Sam sighed, sprinkling cheese on the spaghetti. "I know you don't like Cavenger. I don't really like him much myself. He's got his own reasons why he didn't turn out to be a very nice human being, but he pays our bills."

"We saw the guns and harpoons," Zaidee said, wiping a mustache of milk from her upper lip. "He doesn't care if he kills the creatures, does he?"

"Probably not," Dr. Sam said. "He's got a whole lot of money and ego tied up in this . . . "

"Dad, do you think it's your job to help him do whatever he wants with the plesiosaurs?" Loch asked.

Dr. Sam got up and grabbed a bottle of beer out of the refrigerator. "Loch, one of those creatures killed somebody."

"But you don't know why," Loch said. "They've kept out of everybody's way for centuries, until Cavenger barged in here with his fleet of boats and nets to corner them. In a situation like that, any animal would turn and attack."

"Son, these are not any animal."

"You're right." Zaidee spoke up, moving to sit next to her brother. "These are totally incredible living things that haven't been seen for millions of years."

"The one that attacked was defending itself," Loch said. "Dad, these creatures might be a lot smarter than you think. They could have thoughts and feelings—"

"You don't know that," Dr. Sam said.

"What I do know is that they're something rare and mind-boggling. That used to be enough for you, before you went to work for Cavenger," Loch said.

"Yes!" Zaidee agreed.

Dr. Sam slid back into his seat, silently eating his spaghetti. "Dad," Loch went on, "when you were in research and went down in diving bells, you'd come home and sit around the table with Mom and us, and you'd tell us about everything you'd seen. You loved your work. You'd do a thirty-five-hundred-foot dive in a bell and see all kinds of things. You'd be jumping out of your skin with excitement for days. Don't you remember?"

"Yes, Daddy." Zaidee remembered how happy they all had been as a family.

"You saw underwater volcanos and towers of black coral," Loch reminded Dr. Sam. "And once you saw a rare octopus that slid out of its cave. You said the octopus saw you, that its emotions made it change from red to blue to green. You recorded sights never seen before by anyone, and you stayed up all night to write about them. You saw a fish in the Mariana Trench with lights on its tail. You didn't call it a monstrosity—you said it was like a forbidden glimpse into the secret workroom of God, like it was proof that God wasn't clumsy or had lapses of skill, that everything alive no matter how freaky and frightening had some kind of purpose. Dad, don't you remember all that?"

Dr. Sam did remember.

"You used to laugh a lot," Zaidee said.

"Right," Loch agreed. "All of life was like a big adventure. You weren't afraid of Cavenger or keeping a job or anything."

Zaidee agreed. "And you were a lot more fun."

Dr. Sam pushed his plate away from him. "There's one thing you both have to understand. I'm very grateful I've got my job. I never told you, but the medical insurance didn't cover all the hospital expenses when your mother got sick. I didn't want you to worry, but there were funeral expenses, too. I was really strapped. I'm just starting to see the light at the end of the tunnel."

"I'm sorry, Dad," Loch said.

Zaidee took her father's hand. "I'm sorry, too," she said. "But Daddy, we've got to know your answer to our question."

"Yes," Loch agreed. "I mean, suppose one of the creatures just happened to be swimming by *The Revelation*, and Cavenger ordered you to go to the harpoon gun and shoot the thing. Would you?"

Dr. Sam got up, threw the rest of his dinner in the garbage. He had never lied to his kids before, and he wasn't about to start now. "I'm paid to follow orders," he said. "End of discussion. Now, what was it you guys had to tell me today on the yacht?"

Zaidee and Loch looked at each other.

"Nothing," Zaidee said.

"Right," Loch agreed. "Nothing."

➤

Zaidee was asleep by the time Dr. Sam went in to say good night to his son. Loch was sitting up in his bed, surrounded by his drawings of the Waheela, Tazelwurm, and the other cryptids. He was putting the finishing touches on a drawing of the Rogue.

"That's a good sketch," Dr. Sam said.

"Thanks."

"It's got a lot of detail. I didn't notice the crustacean jaw formation, or the cavities on its snout."

"I guess I had a closer look," Loch said.

Dr. Sam sat on the edge of his son's bed.

He saw another sketch Loch had already finished and picked it up. "What's this?"

"Nothing," Loch said. He usually got around to telling his father everything he and Zaidee did, even if it was something Dr. Sam had forbidden. This time he didn't like the feeling in his gut that he couldn't trust his father enough to tell him about Wee Beastie and the waterfall.

"It looks like a young plesiosaur," Dr. Sam said, studying the drawing.

"I figured since they've been around over a million years, they probably had some kids along the way." Loch took the sketch back. "Dad, they've got some kind of nostrils or blowholes. That means they're mammals, right? They've got to surface to breathe?"

"They're reptiles," Dr. Sam said, "but they might have evolved a system to filter air out of water through an auxiliary gill system. There's one type of South American frog can stay underwater its whole life because it's capable of breathing through its skin."

The phone rang, and Dr. Sam went out to the kitchen to answer it. Loch overheard his father's brief utterings of "yes" into the phone and knew he had to be talking with Cavenger.

"What's up?" Loch asked, coming out to the kitchen.

Dr. Sam opened another can of beer. "Cavenger got the keys and code for the salmon grid. Wants me to check it out in the morning, make sure some novice from State Fish and Game doesn't suddenly feel like running a test and opening the grid. It'd give the plesiosaurs clear sailing straight back to Lake Champlain."

"What's with that grid?" Loch wanted to know. "Why'd they build it in the first place?"

"Half the salmon spawning grounds in the country have been wrecked by damming and mill operations," Dr. Sam said, sitting back in the nook. "Now they're having a lot of success getting salmon to swim back up rivers. The grid acts as a kind of big fish ladder and man-made spawning ground."

➣

Dr. Sam got up at dawn and set out in the Volvo. Loch and Zaidee were still asleep when the phone rang at nine. Loch jumped up and grabbed it.

"Hello?" Loch said, trapping the phone in

the crook of his neck as he rubbed the sleep from his eyes.

"Did I wake you?" Sarah asked.

"I guess so," Loch admitted.

Zaidee staggered by, heading for the bathroom. "Oh, God, it's her, isn't it?" she muttered. "I'm warning you, don't trust anybody who wears four-inch-high clogs."

Loch motioned his sister to zipper her mouth. "Were you able to get any wheels?" Loch asked.

"One of the company jeeps," Sarah said. "I'll be right over."

"Bring your snorkel mask and fins."

"What for?"

"You'll find out," Loch said. He hung up, grabbed a glass of orange juice from the refrigerator, and went to the open bathroom door. Zaidee was foaming at the mouth with toothpaste and glaring at him.

"I think we've got to trust her," Loch said. "We're really going to need the jeep."

"If that spoiled brat does anything to hurt Wee Beastie"—Zaidee gagged, spitting her toothpaste out into the sink—"she's one dead dork."

PURSUIT

Sarah drove the jeep off the main base, pulled onto the south lake road, and shoved the stick shift into high gear. She was traveling at a good clip when she spotted Loch and Zaidee walking toward her on the shoulder of the road. She waited until she was close, then braked the jeep hard, screeching it to a stop next to them.

"What's up?" Sarah asked, peering over the top of her favorite sunglasses.

"First stop is North Alburg," Loch said, grabbing the roll bar and swinging himself onto the seat next to her. "The Grand Union."

Zaidee spotted the double Gs on the thick

silver rims of Sarah's glasses. "Nice shades," Zaidee remarked, as she got into the back.

"Thanks." Sarah threw the jeep back into gear and picked up speed along the south road until the fork to North Alburg. There she turned left and headed straight over Snake Mountain.

"Can I drive?" Zaidee asked, the fringe of her bob rippling in the breeze.

Sarah rolled her eyes at Loch. "Is she kidding?"

"I know how to drive," Zaidee said, insulted. "My dad lets me drive the Volvo all the time."

"In circles around the trailer," Loch kidded.

"It's still driving," Zaidee said. She spotted a canvas pocket behind the front seat and lifted its flap. "Hey, you've got a CB radio."

"All the company jeeps have them," Sarah said.

"Great." Zaidee perked up. "I could use a little entertainment." She took the CB out, pulled up its telescopic antenna, and flipped the power switch. There was a lot of static as she turned the tuner knob. Finally, the voices of a couple of truckers came in loud and clear.

"Hello," Zaidee said into the mike, pressing the broadcast button. "Hello. This is The Big Z, The Big Z . . . "

Nobody answered.

In twenty minutes they were over the mountain and in the small town of North Alburg. Sarah slowed the jeep as they traveled down the main street past a black-and-white-shuttered church with a high steeple, a post office that doubled as a newsstand, and a Mobil gas station. At the very end of the street were the huge glass windows of the Grand Union supermarket. Sarah turned the jeep left into the front lot and parked.

"What are you getting?" Sarah asked.

"You'll see," Loch said, getting out.

"You're both acting very strange, is all I can say," Sarah told Loch. "Very strange."

Sarah followed Loch and Zaidee inside. Loch grabbed an empty grocery cart and pushed it toward the back of the store. He stopped at the fish department. A man in a white smock was busy stocking an iced counter.

"You're the manager?" Loch asked.

"That's me." The man smiled.

"I called this morning from Lake Alban,

about buying fish," Loch said. "Remember?"

Sarah thought she was hearing things. "You're getting fish?"

"Yes, fish." Zaidee emphasized "fish."

"Like I told you," the manager said to Loch, "our new delivery comes in tonight, so you can have a good break on what's left."

If there was one thing Loch knew, it was all the different kinds of freshwater and saltwater fish. "Give me three of the sea bass," he told the manager as he moved along the counter with its neat display of fish laid out on the ice bed. The manager tore off a big piece of waxed paper, laid it on the scale, and started piling the fish on it.

"I guess we can use a half dozen fluke and mackerel, right?" Loch asked Zaidee.

"Sure," Zaidee agreed.

"What do you want so much fish for?" Sarah asked, looking really confused.

"Didn't you ever wake up in the morning and get a yen for something?" Zaidee asked, savoring the grimace on Sarah's face.

"Give us a couple of bluefish and a half dozen salmon," Loch told the manager. "And you might as well throw in a few squid."

Zaidee spotted a monkfish at the end of the counter. "We definitely need this!" she said, picking up the fish and rushing it to the scale.

"That is so ugly," Sarah said.

Zaidee relished the expression on Sarah's face. "Oh, and we need that big one," Zaidee cried, seeing a really large striped bass. She whisked it up with her two hands and sailed it right by Sarah's face.

"Nasty!" Sarah yelled. "Get it away!"

Zaidee placed the fish on the scale as Loch thrust his hand into his pocket to check exactly how much money they'd been able to scrape together from their allowances. "How much so far?" Loch asked the manager.

"What do you say to forty bucks for everything?" the manager asked.

"Great," Loch agreed.

"I don't want those disgusting things stinking up the jeep," Sarah complained.

"No problem," the manager told her. He double-wrapped the fish, stuck them in a large black plastic bag with a scoop of ice, and stapled a price ticket to the top of the bag.

"Thanks," Loch said, as he lifted it into the shopping cart and started up the aisle to the checkout counter. Zaidee spotted a box of Fruity Pebbles and added it to the cart.

Sarah waited until they were outside in the parking lot before she let it all out. "What's with the fish?"

"We need to show you," Loch said, swinging the bag into the back of the jeep. "Let me drive, okay?"

Sarah tossed him the keys.

"I can handle a stick shift." Zaidee spoke up.

"Forget it," Sarah said.

Zaidee climbed in next to the fish. She sulked, then opened the box of Fruity Pebbles as they pulled out of the lot and headed out of town. On the way back over Snake Mountain, Zaidee wanted to go on record. "My *brother* needs to show you something," she clarified for Sarah. "I don't."

"Show me what?" Sarah pressed.

"We found something we don't want your father to know about," Loch said. "You've got to promise not to tell him. Not for a while anyway."

"Just tell me," Sarah demanded. "I can't listen this slowly!"

"Promise you won't tell your father!" Zaidee insisted.

"I promise. What is it?"

"You'll see," Loch said.

"Eeeeeeh!" Sarah screamed. "You're both driving me nuts."

➤

When they reached the Lake Alban fork, Loch turned right on the south road. A few miles up, Zaidee spotted the sign they were looking for: FISH CONSERVATION PROJECT. The tires spun up a cloud of dust as Loch turned the jeep hard onto the dirt road and began the steep climb to the top.

"The grid's up here," he said.

"The shocks on this thing aren't great, you know," Sarah warned, holding on to her sunglasses as the jeep hit bump after bump. "What's with this grid, anyway?"

"My dad says it acts like a dam, but it's not," Loch explained, as the road snaked by the main stream, which flowed down from the lake. "It's like a long series of steps, which lets the water run down them. It kills the logging operations, but lets the salmon come up from Champlain."

They drove around a final curve and saw
the control bunker at the very top of the ridge.
There was no sign of the Volvo. Loch had
counted on his father having finished his early-
morning inspection of the controls.

"This is awesome," Sarah said as Loch
pulled the jeep in close to the hillside and
stopped beside the waterfall. He turned off the
engine, got out, and lugged the bag of fish to
the edge of the pool.

"Get your fins on," Loch told Sarah.

"Me too," Zaidee said, grabbing her
snorkling equipment.

"No, Zaidee," Loch said. "It'll be better if
it's just Sarah and me down there for a while.
Then it'll be your turn."

Zaidee's eyes opened wide. "That's discrim-
ination."

"Trust me," Loch said. He didn't want to
take the chance of confusing the creature by
having too many of them in the water at the
same time.

Zaidee kicked the back of the front seat of
the jeep and stuffed another handful of Fruity
Pebbles in her mouth. "Five minutes," she said.
"That's all I'm waiting."

Sarah took her sunglasses off and stuck them in the glove compartment. Zaidee grunted and tried the CB again. She flipped through the frequencies as Loch and Sarah stripped to their bathing suits.

Loch reached into the bag of fish and started to lift out one of the big fish.

"Better take a little one first," Zaidee suggested. "Like an appetizer."

"You're right," Loch said, exchanging the big bass for a mackerel. He held the mackerel by the tail, lay down on the slab of granite at the edge of the pool, and dangled the fish below the surface of the water.

"Feeding otters, is that what this is all about?" Sarah asked, struggling to get her fins on. "You found a family of otters, right?"

Loch didn't answer. He let go of the fish and let it drift down toward the deep, clear bottom of the pool.

"Follow me," Loch said. He slid into the water, put his mask on, and dove for the bottom. Sarah put her mask on and went after him.

Zaidee immediately took Sarah's sunglasses out of the glove compartment and tried them on. She checked herself in the rearview mirror.

Not bad, she had to admit.

Zaidee got out of the jeep and lifted the huge striped bass out of the fish bag. She struggled to hold it as she walked around the edge of the pool. "Wee Beastie," she called. "Look what Zaidee's got for you."

It was in the deep end of the pool that Loch first heard the anguished cries. Today among the rocks and clusters of water plants there was no haunting, unearthly music. The sounds now were frantic, stabbing. Sarah pointed to her ears, signaling that she, too, could hear them. Loch swam deeper toward the shadowy forest of water plants, but the sounds seemed to be coming from his right. He and Sarah turned and saw Wee Beastie in the turmoil where the waterfall plunged into the pool. The creature was shrieking, oblivious of them, thrusting itself upward over and over again into the onslaught of falling water.

Sarah's eyes opened wide in shock. She felt as if she were back in the nightmare of the lake again. What little air was left in her lungs burst from her and she kicked swiftly for the surface.

Loch followed her up, and they threw themselves out of the water and onto the slab of rock.

Sarah gasped, ripping off her mask and spitting out water. "That's what you wanted to show me!" She started screaming at Loch. "That!"

"He got washed down here from the lake," Loch said.

"You made me go into the water with that monstrosity?" Sarah shouted, feeling her body start to shake. "How could you?"

"He's not a monster!" Zaidee said, outraged. She set the big bass down. "We swam and played with him all day yesterday. He's a lot nicer and smarter than some people we know."

Loch went to put his arm around Sarah, but she shook him off. "You know what that is going to grow up into as well as I do."

"We didn't know you were going to freak out," Zaidee said, taking off Sarah's sunglasses and tossing them back into the glove compartment.

"Sarah," Loch said, "he's a fantastic creature—"

"Look, I don't know about you, but I can

still feel Erdon's blood on my arms," Sarah said, heading for the jeep.

Loch grabbed her arm, stopping her. "You can't tell your father or he'll kill him."

"It looks like it's doing a good job of killing itself," Sarah said.

"Wait," Loch said.

Sarah reached the jeep and pounded its right fender three times with her fist. Loch let her blow off steam.

"What's the matter with Wee Beastie?" Zaidee wanted to know.

"He's freaking out," Loch said.

"Wee Beastie?" Sarah cried out in disbelief. "You've named it like it's your pet dog?"

"What's he doing?" Zaidee asked.

"He's crying, making those really terrible sounds like when you take a kitten away from its mother," Loch said. "It looks like he's trying to swim back up the waterfall, like he's trying to get back to his mother—"

"And the rest of the flesh-eating monsters," Sarah finished his sentence.

"He's not like that," Loch said, going to Sarah. "I guess we should have told you, but you wouldn't have even gone in then." Sarah let him put his arm around her. "I'm sorry."

"It's too late for that," Sarah said.

"Can't you just trust me?" Loch asked. Sarah looked down from his stare, moved away, and pounded the fender again. "Trust me," he repeated. "Let's go back down."

"I don't want to," she said.

"For crying out loud, don't beg her." Zaidee spoke up.

"Sarah," Loch said, reaching out for her hand. "I'm going to need your help." He led her back to the edge of the pool and handed her her mask. She made a face but took it. Loch put his mask on and slid into the water. Finally, Sarah lowered herself into the water next to him. Loch kicked up his feet, diving for the bottom with Sarah behind him. This time they swam straight for the creature, its cries cutting through the rumble of the falling water. Loch reached Wee Beastie first. He stretched out his hand and touched it. Sarah hung back as it turned to look at them.

"It's okay, boy . . . okay," Loch said, his words muffled and carried out in an exhale of bubbles that rose across the face of his mask. He stroked the creature's head, trying to turn it from the churning water. Loch signaled Sarah away, back toward the dead mackerel that lay on the bottom of the pool. He followed her. The creature watched them. Loch put the fish in Sarah's hands and had her hold it out toward Wee Beastie. Finally, the creature stopped its crying. Slowly it turned from the falls and swam toward them. It stopped a few feet away, staring at Sarah and the fish. Loch took Sarah's hands and opened them so the mackerel floated slowly downward. Before it touched the bottom of the pool, Wee Beastie reared its head back, then snapped forward, flashing its astounding mouthful of teeth. Sarah screamed beneath the water, backing away fast as Wee Beastie lurched again and again until only a few remaining scales from the mackerel settled like snowflakes.

➤

It took several dives with more fish before Loch and Sarah surfaced with Wee Beastie at their sides.

"Wee Beastie!" Zaidee cried out, dropping down on the ledge. The creature lifted his head for her to pet him, and she rolled the huge striped bass into the water for him. His teeth flew at it, shredding and eating it in seconds.

"Isn't he cute?" she asked Sarah.

Sarah looked at Zaidee like she was out of her mind. "If I ever saw cute, this is it."

"We have visitors," Zaidee told Loch, tossing Wee Beastie another fish.

"Where?" Loch asked.

"Listen," Zaidee told him, pointing up toward the ridge. "I was also able to tune them in on the CB. Sounds like they're zeroing in on something."

Loch and Sarah pulled themselves out of the water and yanked off their fins. Loch had figured Cavenger would eventually get men to check out the lakeshore just as he had done, but he hadn't thought it would be this soon. They could hear the voices floating down to them from the lake. Men's voices. The sound of boat motors. Splashing. "You guys keep feeding Wee Beastie," Loch instructed, dumping the fish into a pile on the rock. "I'll check it out."

Loch ran across the spillway from the pond and onto the path next to the grid. He started up toward the bunker, his bare feet digging into the mixture of small stones and clay. The sounds and voices of the men grew louder as he climbed. At the top of the ridge he saw them.

The converted PT boat was anchored offshore above the area where Loch had seen the bottom scrapings. Two of the smaller fleet boats idled close by, with John Randolph and Cavenger's dive master shouting instructions to a half dozen motley frogmen who were diving, searching the area. There were shouts from other men on the shore where pines and thick brush blocked Loch's view. He knew they had found the set of smaller scrapings and the underground spillway.

Loch raced back down the hill as fast as he could.

"What's going on?" Sarah wanted to know when she saw him coming.

"Your father's got Randolph with divers," Loch said, working to catch his breath. "They've closed in on the trail. We've got to get Wee Beastie out of here."

Zaidee and Loch looked at Sarah to see if she was with them. "All right," Sarah said, "what should we do?"

"Get him into the jeep," Loch said.

"No," Zaidee cried. She pointed down the hill. "Look!"

A trail of dust was rising from the curving,

narrow dirt road. Another company jeep with more of Cavenger's men in it was heading up. Loch looked toward the grid, then to the pool. The creature's head was out of the water. It was making cheerful sounds out of the breathing holes on its snout and staring at the rest of the big pile of squid and fish. Loch grabbed a bluefish and held it out to the creature. "Come on, fellah, you've got to come with us." Loch moved around the edge of the pond to the spillway. Wee Beastie followed Loch, swimming along the rim of the pool. Loch tossed him the fish.

"The spillway is too shallow for him," Loch shouted. "We have to help."

Loch jumped into the pool next to Wee Beastie, as the creature snapped up the last morsels of the largest bluefish. Loch tried bracing his legs against the side of the pool to lift Wee Beastie into the flow of the spillway, but the creature was too slippery and heavy. Zaidee and Sarah rushed to get a grip, carefully sliding their arms under Wee Beastie's two front fins. Wee Beastie didn't seem to mind. He kept making cheerful noises and looking longingly over his shoulder at the pile of fish as they eased him up. Finally, he was out of the pool and into the shallow spillway.

A cry came from the top of the waterfall. They looked up to see the first frogman being washed over the falls and plunging downward. Two more terrified-looking divers were swept over after him.

Loch was out of the pool now. He pushed Wee Beastie along the wash, while Sarah and Zaidee continued to help glide him along by his fins. In another few feet the spillway was deeper and steeper, and they were able to move the creature faster.

"Let go," Loch ordered Zaidee. "Delay them!"

Zaidee understood and turned away as the water rushed over her ankles. She headed back to the jeep, while Sarah and Loch slid quickly with the creature into the shin-deep top waters of the grid.

The frogmen surfaced in the pool. Zaidee knew it would take them a few moments to get their bearings. Finally, when they looked to the shore, all they could see was a small girl with short bobbed hair sitting in the back of a company jeep. She had her feet up and crossed, and was munching from a box of Fruity Pebbles.

"Hi." Zaidee waved to them. "Nice day for a swim."

The frogmen swam to the edge of the pool and pulled themselves out onto the granite ledge. They saw the pile of wet snorkel equipment thrown into the back of the jeep. "Who's out here with you?" one of the frogmen demanded to know.

"A couple of friends. We're having a picnic." Zaidee smiled. "They're in the woods looking for firewood. Would you like some Fruity Pebbles?"

They noticed the pile of squid and fish on the rock. "What's that?"

"Oh, you know," Zaidee said, "we always say, what's a picnic without roast fish!"

Randolph's voice came roaring from the top of the ridge. He was running down from the bunker, clutching a walkie-talkie and pointing downstream. "Get them!"

The divers turned and spotted Loch and Sarah splashing their way down the grid with a strange black creature. In a second, the frogmen were after them.

The water on the second level of the grid

was knee-deep, sufficient for Wee Beastie to propel himself along beside them like a seal. Loch kept urging him on. "Don't worry, fellah, we're going to make it. Just hang in there. You'll be okay."

But the end of the grid steps looked too far away.

Sarah looked over her shoulder as she pushed ahead. "They're coming!" she yelled. Loch turned and saw the frogmen already in the top of the grid. More men were racing down from the bunker to join Randolph. Loch could only think that if somehow Sarah and he could get Wee Beastie to the last grid step, he would make it over the last obstacle and escape into the deep, swift stream to Lake Champlain.

The frogmen were gaining on them.

"I'm getting exhausted!" Sarah yelled when the water grew still deeper near the end of the fourth step. Here a steel barrier forced the powerful surge of water to cascade down to the next step, a drop of several feet. Wee Beastie couldn't make it over alone. The creature tried to turn from the barrier, to go back toward the pursuers, but Loch and Sarah got behind him again and started to lift him. With a great fluttering of his front fins, finally Wee Beastie went splashing over into the next grid step.

"What is that?" Sarah called as she and Loch dropped down to the lower grid. A rippling of white water lay directly ahead.

"Artificial rapids," Loch called back.

"They look real enough to me!" Sarah gasped as the current pulled her along.

"Look!" Loch yelled, pointing ahead. Beyond the end of the last grid, coming up the stream, was a skiff carrying a crew of armed men. Cavenger must have had a second team searching downstream, and Randolph had ordered it into position with his walkie-talkie.

They were trapped; men were closing from upstream and down.

➤

Back at the waterfall, Zaidee continued to relax in the backseat of the jeep, eating her Fruity Pebbles. Randolph was yelling at her, asking her about the black creature, what it was, what her brother and Sarah were doing with it.

"It's an otter," Zaidee told him, "a big old mutant otter." The more Randolph yelled at her, the more she kept her attention on two things: the sight of her buddies trapped in the grid and the keys hanging in the jeep's ignition. The second company jeep made it up the hill and screeched to a halt next to Randolph. Four burly men in fatigues leaped out to join in the chase. It was getting very unfair, Zaidee felt. Then the huge military helicopter lifted over the ridge with a roar. As far as Zaidee was concerned, that was downright mean. That was overkill.

Randolph shouted commands into his walkie-talkie while the chopper hovered above, kicking up great swirls of dust. Zaidee waited until no one was looking at her, then slid into the driver's seat of the jeep and turned the key in the ignition. The jeep started. In a second, she had it in gear. Randolph turned and saw her. "Hey!" he yelled.

"Party on!" Zaidee shouted. She floored the accelerator, making the jeep's wheels spin and tear into the ground. A few of the men ran to stop her, but the wheels gripped, and the jeep shot forward onto the dirt road, heading fast down the hill. Zaidee kept the gear in second. She wanted power with speed.

Below, in the grid, Loch and Sarah had

stopped. There seemed to be no point in going forward or in turning back. The frogmen and Randolph's crew were bearing down on them through the grid and along the shore path. The men in the skiff closed from downstream.

"I'm sorry, fellah," Loch told Wee Beastie. The creature had heard the sounds of the strange men and had begun to tremble.

"Can't we do anything?" Sarah cried out.

"I don't think so," Loch said sadly.

Suddenly, there was a screech of brakes on the left bank and a cloud of dust as a vehicle skidded to a stop.

"Move it!" Zaidee yelled.

Loch, Sarah—even Wee Beastie—turned, surprised by Zaidee's sudden arrival at the wheel of the jeep. "Way to go!" Loch shouted. They pushed their way through the rushing water to the cement slab that lined the bank. Sarah climbed onto a set of rungs, clutching the creature around his neck. Loch, struggling to keep his footing in the strong current, lifted Wee Beastie as high as he could, but it wasn't enough. Zaidee jumped out of the jeep, ran to the edge, and reached to grab one of Wee Beastie's fins.

The men running down the path were nearly upon them. The second jeep, with Randolph, was coming fast down the hill road.

Then, with one last effort from all of them, Wee Beastie was out of the grid. The three of them lifted him into the back of the jeep. Loch jumped behind the wheel and threw the jeep into gear while Sarah and Zaidee held on to the creature. Three of Randolph's men came running from the grid path and tried to grab onto the jeep as it moved forward. Wee Beastie snapped his head back, then lunged forward, letting his awesome cluster of teeth snap out at them. The men screamed, pulling their arms away fast before they could be bitten off. The jeep gained speed, shooting forward through the last treacherous curves of the hillside before racing out onto the paved south road.

The pursuit jeep with Randolph had fallen behind, but the enormous helicopter swooped down quickly as though from nowhere, its shadow falling on them like that of a great, brown wasp.

SUNDOWN

The helicopter stayed low, practically on top of the speeding jeep as it hit an open stretch of the road. A gruff voice on the helicopter's speakers blared down at them to stop. Finally, the road snaked under a cover of tall pines and birch.

"We'll be lucky if we make it as far as the trailer," Loch said. "Then we'll be cornered."

"The lake!" Zaidee cried out. "We've got to at least get him into the lake!"

➤

The creature made its noises loud and clear. CLICK CLICK . . .

CLACK CLICK CLACK . . .

"What's with him?" Sarah asked.

"He makes those noises whenever he thinks we're going to leave him," Zaidee explained. "He always wants to stay with us."

CLICK CLACK . . .

➤

By the time the pursuit jeep made the turn into the Perkins camp, Randolph had already radioed the helicopter to set down in the field near the duck pond. Six armed men were already marching toward the jeep parked at the edge of the lake. Loch, Sarah, and Zaidee stood next to it waiting for them.

"Hey," Loch yelled at the men, "you're trespassing!"

"Where is it?" Randolph demanded, striding up to check out the jeep.

"I told you it was only an otter," Zaidee said, ticked off. "A mutant ninja otter."

"We put it back in the lake," Loch said.

"Search the grounds," Randolph ordered his men. Half of the men spread out over the dock and lakefront, the other half moved to check the grounds and duck pond. Randolph singled Sarah out. "We know what it is. What did you do with it?"

"Where's my father?" Sarah asked.

"He's on his way," Randolph said. He turned away from them, moving quickly to the trailer.

"Hey," Loch yelled, "keep out of there!"

Randolph ignored him, drew his gun, and went into the trailer. By the time Loch went in after him, Randolph was already past the pile of junk on the living-room floor and moving down the narrow and dark back hallway. He saw a closed door and reached out for the knob.

"Hey, don't open that," Loch shouted. "That's my room!"

Randolph opened the door fast.

"*EEEEEEEEE!*" Randolph screamed as the head of the hideous cryptid, its mouth gaping, came flying at him. He saw the faces of another dozen snarling monsters and began shooting. He had gotten off all six shots before he realized he had blasted half of Loch's cryptozoo collection.

Loch threw up his hands in disgust. "You're a geek!" he yelled at Randolph. "A grade-A, U.S. prime geek!"

Loch came out of the trailer as Dr. Sam and Cavenger pulled up in the Volvo. Dr. Sam had heard the gunshots. "What happened?"

Loch shrugged as he sat down on the trailer steps. "Randolph just assassinated my bedroom."

➤

Sunlight reflected from the back of Cavenger's balding head as he strolled away from all the shouting and accusations. His small, deep-set eyes stared out toward the lake while Dr. Sam conducted the interrogation. Loch, Zaidee, and Sarah stuck to their story that they had been at the grid feeding an otter and hadn't wanted Randolph and his men to shoot it.

"That was no otter," Randolph kept repeating.

"It doesn't matter," Cavenger said finally. "Whatever it was, we'll net it on tomorrow's sweep." He turned to Dr. Sam. "Let's go. We have a lot of work to finish at the base."

Cavenger put Sarah in the back of the Volvo and got into the front passenger seat. Dr. Sam got behind the wheel and started the engine. He rolled down the window for a parting shot at Randolph. "You stay off my property."

"Your property?" Cavenger laughed. "I pay the rents around here."

As usual, Dr. Sam said nothing. He just drove off.

Randolph and his men left right after Dr. Sam and Cavenger, leaving Loch and Zaidee alone at the camp. Zaidee walked out and sat on the rinky-dink dock at the spot where they had put Wee Beastie back into the lake. There was no sign of the creature anywhere. She started to cry. Loch walked over to her and sat down.

"Don't, Zaidee," Loch said. "We're not going to give up."

"They're going to catch Wee Beastie tomorrow," Zaidee said. "They're going to kill him."

"No," Loch said. "There's got to be something we can do. We have to think of something . . . "

"Wee Beastie could still be right out there," Zaidee said. "Maybe he didn't swim very far."

"He'll be okay," Loch said. "I'm sure he's finding his mother."

He hadn't meant to say the word "mother." It was a word they both tried to use as little as possible.

"They'll trap them all tomorrow," Zaidee wept. "Wee Beastie will be harpooned or shot or caught in those big metal nets and die."

Loch stood and looked out past the shallows to the dark edge of the deep water. By now the shadows of the pines were thrust far out onto the lake as the sun began to drop behind the mountains. "You're right," he told Zaidee. "Wee Beastie could still be hanging around. I have to look for him."

Zaidee stopped crying. "Are you going out in the boat?"

"No," Loch said. He turned and climbed the slope to the U-Haul.

Zaidee ran after him. "I want to go with you," she said.

"You can't," Loch said. "If I meet one of the big ones, we'll . . . have problems."

"Don't go," Zaidee pleaded. "The sun's going down. It's too dangerous."

"I'll be okay." Loch opened the combination lock and threw open the heavy metal door of the truck. He jumped up inside and lifted the canvas cover from the Jet Ski. He moved the ski out onto the truck elevator platform and lowered it to the ground. Zaidee helped him push it to the lake.

"I've got to get something," Zaidee said, heading up to the trailer while Loch fueled the

Jet Ski from the boat's reserve tank. By now the shadows from the mountains themselves began to march on the lake. Only the sky was afire with the stark reds and yellows of sunset.

Zaidee ran back down as Loch started the Jet Ski. "Here," she said, thrusting the laptop at him. "This will let you know if he's around." Her voice dropped. "If anything's around."

"Great," Loch said. He flipped the laptop open, turned it on, and strapped it onto the seat behind him. He'd have to twist around to look at it, but it was better than nothing.

"I want to go with you," Zaidee said.

"Not this time," Loch told her.

"I could hold the laptop and watch the screen."

"You'd be too heavy. I need the speed."

Zaidee knew he was right. "Well, you are going to need this," she said, reaching out to the computer and bringing Crashers up on the screen. "If Wee Beastie sees you, maybe he'll follow you back."

"Maybe," Loch said, tousling his sister's hair. He kicked the ski into gear and started away from the dock.

"Be careful," Zaidee called after him.

Loch skimmed slowly across the shallows out onto the black water. He knew it would be light for ten or fifteen minutes more. A breeze was coming down from the north. The wisps of the night fog were already forming in the center of the lake.

He turned to check the game screen. There were no telltale static lines.

Farther out the breeze was stronger, whisking off the tops of the waves into streaks of white. He saw a floating log off to his left and another to his right.

Why so many logs? he thought. Any logs that had been washed out of the log pond during the storm should have all drifted to the south shore by now.

He kept his speed low, calling around him, "Hey, fellah, it's all clear now. . . . Where are you, little fellah?" He put on the ski's headlight and leaned forward to check the surface ahead. "It's safe now, Wee Beastie," he called into the breeze. "All the bad guys are gone—"

Loch turned sharply to avoid another log. He thought he had missed it entirely, but the motor on the ski stalled. He tried the automatic start. The motor turned over right away, but when he put it into gear it sputtered and stalled again. He knew the symptoms. It meant a branch or weeds were caught in the front intake. Whatever, he'd have to get into the water to clear it. "Nasty," he moaned as he checked to make certain the ignition was turned off and the motor in neutral.

There still were no static lines on the laptop as he slid over the side into the dark, cold water.

The chill of the deep lake was numbing even in summer. He trod water and held on to the ski's running board to keep his head above the surface. With his right hand he reached around to the front of the ski and blindly felt below the waterline for the clogged intake, as he had done many times before. He located the clog and pulled at it. Part of it came loose, and he lifted it into the headlight to get a good look at it. It was a leafy stem of a water plant. He threw the stem clear and reached back underwater. The rest of the clog seemed less leafy, as though it were soft, thin lake grass attached to a clump. He pulled the clump back and forth, trying to loosen it from the intake. Whatever it was, it was really jammed. Loch had to jump the grip of his left hand from the running board to the front plastic bumper to get the leverage he needed.

Finally, the clump loosened. It was heavier than he expected, but he floated it to the surface, closer to the blazing light of the headlamp. At first he thought it might be some child's waterlogged ball caught in the lake grass, but as he lifted it into the light he saw a pair of eyes in a bloated, half-eaten human face staring out at him. The bottom half of the mouth was gone, leaving two gold front teeth to protrude and shine down from the upper slab of bone.

Loch yelled and threw the grisly head of Jesse Sanderson as far away from him as he could. Then he pulled himself quickly through the water, grasped the running board, and hauled himself back up. He noticed a thick, jagged line, growing larger, cutting across the game screen. He swung himself squarely on the front of the seat and pressed the start button.

CHUG. CHUGGG. The motor coughed but wouldn't kick over. He turned the headlight off, letting the full power of the battery go to the starter. It was very dark now. The screen of the laptop glowed eerily behind him. He pressed the start button. The motor gurgled and chugged again.

Loch smelled gasoline. He had flooded the engine. It would have to sit a second.

The static line on the laptop filled the screen now.

Loch heard the sound of water moving in front of him. It was too dark to see, but he felt the ski undulate from what seemed to be a single large wave. He moved his hand to the headlight switch. Battery or no battery, he had to see what had surfaced. He flicked the switch. The light cut through the night. A huge black mass lay in front of him like a small island. Above it rose the massive head and glaring yellow eyes of the Rogue.

Loch froze. His heart felt like it was going to explode in his chest. He told himself the creature wouldn't attack him unless it felt threatened.

"Hi, big fellah," Loch found himself muttering as the Rogue moved his snout closer to the front of the ski. "I'm not going to hurt you. . . ."

The Rogue nudged the ski and began to open his mouth. Loch couldn't take his eyes off the huge chasm lined with great pointed daggers. He tried again to convince himself that if he didn't make any sudden movements, the creature would let him go.

Then his instincts won out. Loch's hand crept to the starter button.

"Now! Now!" Loch yelled, holding the starter button down. The engine roared. In a split second Loch had the ski in gear as the beast's head pulled back. Loch spun the ski around, flying away just as the beast's mouth shot forward like the front of a roaring train.

Loch's eyes fixed on the lights of the trailer and dock as he gave the ski full throttle. He heard sounds behind him but didn't dare look back. He was still a few hundred yards from shore. He saw himself bearing down on a log and jerked the ski to the left to avoid hitting it.

Now he was close enough to see Zaidee on the pier. "Hurry!" she was screaming. "It's after you!"

A hundred yards to go.

Loch leaned his body forward and low to cut the wind resistance.

"Faster!" Zaidee called out to him.

A big log lay directly in front of him. There was no way he could avoid it. He braced himself and held the ski straight. The ski hit and was airborne. Loch stayed on and landed the ski back in the water. He was in the shallows now.

Zaidee screamed, "It's still coming!"

Loch turned, staring back with terror to see the creature erupting with a great roar from the water, the thrust from its powerful fins sending it hurtling toward Loch. Loch looked for a weapon—the laptop!—grabbed it, and threw it. The beast's teeth snapped closed, exploding the screen and case, which came whizzing back over his head.

"Oh my God," Zaidee cried, running off the pier as fast as her legs would carry her.

Loch shot up on the shore with the ski, leaped off, and ran up the slope with Zaidee.

It took them a long while to realize that the beast had stopped, and that it had returned to the deep.

Loch collapsed on the ground. Near him

he found the shattered case of the laptop. He picked the case up and ran his fingers along the jagged edges made by the Rogue's teeth.

"This is a megabyte," he told Zaidee. "A real megabyte."

NIGHT

Zaidee was asleep by the time Dr. Sam got home. Loch had decided not to tell her about finding Jesse Sanderson's head in the lake. He knew she'd been through enough to give her nightmares for a very long time as it was. Nor would he tell his father about Jesse. There was no need, just yet, for others to know what had happened to the town drunk who swaggered around Lake Alban with a shotgun. The beasts were already hated enough.

By midnight a half-moon had risen over the mountains, and the dangers of the lake faded before its vast beauty. Loch waited up for his father, staring out the window at the sweep of stars that lay suspended in the dark velvet of the northern sky. Only the fragile cries from distant loons broke the silence of the night.

"What the hell was going on today?" Dr. Sam wanted to know when he came in, his face drawn. He grabbed a bottle of beer and swung into the dining nook next to Loch. "Why didn't you tell me what you'd found?"

"You were too busy."

"Don't throw that back in my face."

"We found what I drew—a young plesiosaur," Loch said. "That's what we tried to tell you yesterday."

"A juvenile?"

"Yes."

Dr. Sam took a sip of his beer. He let the fact sink in, imagining for a moment what he would have done if he had known. "Well, you heard Cavenger. It doesn't make any difference now."

Loch got right to what was on his mind. "He's going to kill them, isn't he?"

"He's hoping to take one alive."

"You don't really believe that, do you?"

"I—"

"Dad, special equipment would have to be built to take any of the big creatures alive," Loch said. "Cavenger wouldn't spend the time—or the money—to do it right. All he's got on *The Revelation* are guns and harpoons. And any young ones are going to die in the nets. You know that!"

"I don't know that—"

Loch hit his fist on the table. "Dad, you do!"

"Don't wake Zaidee," Dr. Sam said.

"I need to talk to you," Loch said, getting up and going outside. Dr. Sam took his beer and went out after him. He caught up to him walking down to the lake.

"The creature I found was frightened and scraped and terrified," Loch went on. "Zaidee and I went into the water with him, and he began to trust us. He's not some kind of stupid fake out of one of Cavenger's lousy magazines. He's real. He's alive. Dad, he's very smart."

"Loch, it's a prehistoric beast—"

"I'm telling you they're all more than just a pack of monsters. The little one makes sounds, like a kind of music. He cries and feels pain. All these creatures, they're just trying to stay alive and be left alone. Life doesn't mean anything to Cavenger, but it's got to mean something to you, Dad. It's got to!"

"You and Zaidee mean something to me—"

"Then don't just stand by and let him slaughter them and stuff them for some stupid museum. This lake has a great treasure! It's more than gold, don't you know that? Don't you?"

"Son," Dr. Sam said, "I don't know why you're trying to defend these beasts. I know I've moved you and Zaidee around a lot . . . you haven't had the chance to have many friends—"

Loch raised his voice. "Don't, Dad! You're not hearing what I'm telling you. Please don't say anything dumb now—"

"What kind of a thing is that to say?" Dr. Sam asked, confused.

Loch turned and started to walk away but then spun to face his father. "Zaidee and I are supposed to look up to you, but we don't. We don't because it's almost like you don't exist anymore, like you've given yourself away piece by piece." Loch trembled as he pointed out at the lake. "We saved one of them. I'm telling you they have feelings and intelligence. At least take the time to know what we know. You think you won't be able to learn anything from them. You're wrong—"

"Look, you're a kid . . ."

"Dad, some fantastic and mind-blowing creatures are trapped out there and you're just standing by, helping to destroy them."

"I only work for Cavenger," Dr. Sam said.

"But you're the grown-ups!" Loch found himself shouting now. "You're supposed to do what's right!"

Dr. Sam looked out at the lake. "Loch, I'm sorry," he said finally, and started back up the slope to the trailer.

Loch ran after him and stopped him. "You have the codes for the grid. You could open it. The creatures could go back where they came from."

"I can't do that," Dr. Sam said.

"You can."

"No."

"What you're saying is you won't."

"You're out of line, son."

Loch curled his fingers into a fist. Dr. Sam saw it as well as the look in his son's eyes. Dr.

Sam turned away and opened the trailer door. He went inside, leaving Loch alone in the night.

➤

Dr. Sam had to leave for the base before dawn. Loch and Zaidee were still sleeping in their rooms, so he scrawled them a note:

> *Good morning!*
> *Please take care of yourselves and stay out of trouble until I get back. I'll make it all up to you. I promise. Camping. A dozen new computer games. Swim with dolphins. A real vacation. You name it.*
>
> *Love, Dad*

The guard was waiting at the encampment gate when Dr. Sam arrived.

"Today's the day," the guard said. Dr. Sam saw the excitement in the guard's eyes.

"Right," Dr. Sam said, then drove on through. He parked near the dock, got out, and headed for *The Revelation*. The thrill of the hunt charged the air as fleet crews and personnel scurried everywhere. The water taxis skimmed between the dock and skiffs like water beetles. A few of the lighter, oldest boats had been

replaced in the search formation by the converted PT and a pair of twenty-six-foot metal-
hull patrol boats hauled overland from Lake
Champlain. The highest security surrounded an
army truck delivering a long gray crate to the
yacht. Dr. Sam followed the crate up the gangplank.

Cavenger was waiting for the crate in the
control room. "Here's what we've been waiting
for," he said as the crew set the crate down
against the far wall.

The mood in the control room was confi-
dent as Emilio and Randolph unpacked several
pieces of heavy-duty artillery. In addition to up-
graded electronics systems, the yacht now carried a half dozen automatic guns, a grenade
launcher, and several explosive-tip spear guns.

Dr. Sam checked the ammunition supply.
"You've got enough explosives aboard to blow
up half the lake."

"We'll use what we have to," Cavenger said.

Emilio checked the sights on the grenade
launcher. "I was certified on this launcher in the
army."

"When?" Dr. Sam asked. "Twenty years
ago?"

Randolph slid a clip into an automatic rifle. "It's like riding a bike," he said. "Just like riding a bike."

>

Loch had heard his father get up that morning and stumble around the trailer to fix his coffee and toast. Loch wanted to get up, go out to the dining nook, and apologize to his dad for his outburst the night before. Instead, he lay on his bed staring at the remains of the cryptids and the sunlight streaming in through the bullet holes in the wall.

When he heard the Volvo drive off, he got up, poured himself a glass of orange juice, and read the note his father had left. The sunshine drew him outside. Barefoot and in his pjs, he walked down to the lake and picked up a handful of pebbles. He sat on the edge of the dock and stared out at the still, glassy surface of the water. One by one he tossed the stones in, watching them splash and send out ever-widening circles. Somewhere out there were Wee Beastie and the giant creatures.

"They're going to try to kill Wee Beastie and the other creatures today, aren't they?" came Zaidee's voice. Loch turned to see his sister in her nightgown munching on a bowl of cereal as she came down the slope.

"Yes," Loch said. He would have lied to her, but he knew she'd see right through him. Cavenger would slaughter every one of the creatures rather than let them get away.

Zaidee sat next to him on the dock and dipped her toes in the water. "Wee Beastie's very smart. They don't know that."

"No, they don't," Loch agreed.

"And if he's just a kid plesiosaur, you can imagine how smart the big ones are," Zaidee added.

Loch saw a long, dark shadow emerging from the black water into the clear shallows. He stood. Zaidee spotted it too and jumped up.

"Oh," Loch said, "it's just another log."

"Right. Another log."

Loch looked to Zaidee. Suddenly, he was fully awake. He jumped up and rushed back toward the trailer.

"Hey, you're thinking what I'm thinking, aren't you?" Zaidee asked, running after him.

Inside, Loch grabbed the phone and dialed Sarah. It rang several times before she answered.

"Are you out of your mind?" Sarah's sleepy voice came out of the receiver. She knew Loch was the only one who'd have the nerve to call so early.

"Do you have to sail with your father today?" Loch asked.

"No."

"Good."

"When do you need the jeep?" Sarah moaned.

"No," Loch said. "A boat."

"You've got a bass boat."

"A bigger one," Loch said. "I think I know where the creatures hide."

➤

By ten A.M. the search fleet was under way, with *The Revelation* setting the pace for the sweep. The PT was first to the yacht's port side, with a new documentary photographer Cavenger had flown in from London. The pair of clanking fishing trawlers flanked the fleet. Both trawlers had let out their full lengths of rusted-steel netting by the time the fleet passed Dr. Sam's trailer camp on the south shore.

Dr. Sam looked up from his console of graphic recorders as they scratched their ink

zigzags onto the rolls of graph paper. Out the
window he could see the motionless specks of
Loch and Zaidee standing on the dock watching
the fleet pass. Loch's words last night repeated
inside him as Dr. Sam caught his reflection in
the glass.

"Sit down," Cavenger ordered him.

"Sorry," Dr. Sam said.

"Today we will be famous," Cavenger
spouted, basking in the glow of the dozen flickering sonar screens. His hands trembled as he
tensed forward in the command chair, looking
to Emilio and Randolph for their assurance.
They smiled and nodded to him.

"This time we're ready for them," Emilio
said.

"Right," Randolph agreed.

At the wheel Haskell kept his eyes straight
ahead.

It was ten minutes after *The Revelation* had
passed the logging mill that the first significant
BLIP hit the screens. By now even Cavenger
had learned to read the difference between a
beaver or a log and their prey.

"I've got one of them," Cavenger said, his
voice cracking with excitement.

"It's very deep," Dr. Sam confirmed. "Deep under us."

Cavenger looked like a ghost in the strobe light. "It's coming up! Give the alert!"

Randolph went on the PA. "Sighting! All crew in place!"

The harpoon team readied the equipment on the bow. A half dozen other crew members with rifles took their positions topside. Emilio got the alert out over the ship's radio. A dozen armed men moved to their stations around the perimeter of the PT.

"It's the big one," Cavenger said, checking the signal.

"Yes, it's big," Dr. Sam confirmed.

"How deep?" Emilio asked.

"Rising from eight hundred feet," Dr. Sam called as the seconds ticked by. "Eight hundred, seven hundred, six hundred fifty . . . "

BLIP, BLIP, BLIP.

"Five hundred feet and closing . . . "

BLIP . . .

Cavenger reached his hands out around the edges of the master screen in front of him like a warlock peering into a cauldron. "We've got this one."

"We won't be able to net it out here," Dr. Sam said.

"No," Cavenger said without looking up. "But we are going to blow its head off. We get the carcass of the first one, then we can worry about netting the others."

Dr. Sam shifted in his seat.

The sonar signal disappeared at three hundred fifty feet.

"What's going on?" Cavenger shouted, turning away from the screens to look at Dr. Sam. "What happened to our signal?"

"Nothing," Dr. Sam said.

Cavenger jumped up to check the graphic recorders. "Get that signal back," he ordered.

"Our sonar is operational," Dr. Sam said, confused. "The creature's disappeared."

"A beast that size doesn't just disappear," Cavenger roared.

There was a mild impact to the boat, enough to throw the frail Cavenger off balance. Emilio grabbed him before he fell.

"What was that?" Cavenger asked.

"We've hit something," Haskell said nervously. He shifted the motor's gears. "We've got power, but it's not engaging the prop."

"Tell everyone to hold their positions," Cavenger ordered Randolph. He got on the radio as Cavenger went to Haskell. "What is going on!" he yelled.

"There must be something wrong with the propeller shaft," Haskell said.

"I think he's right," Emilio agreed.

"We're dead in the water, is that what you're telling me?" Cavenger began to rant.

"We must have hit one of those logs." Captain Haskell's voice cracked in the face of Cavenger's fury. "Probably a sheared cotter pin. We can fix it, but someone's going to have to go down."

Cavenger turned on Randolph. "You're the dive engineer. Go fix it!"

"Mr. Cavenger," Randolph said respectfully, "we had something on the sonar. One of the creatures is somewhere around here."

"No, it isn't," Cavenger said. "Sam said it disappeared, didn't you, Sam?"

"It's not on the sonar," Dr. Sam replied.

"Then it's gone, is that correct?" Cavenger pressed. "Or don't you know what the hell you're talking about?"

"It's gone," Dr. Sam said uneasily.

"Fine," Cavenger told Dr. Sam. "And since you're the great oceanographer, you can buddy Randolph on the dive."

THE DEN
OF THE
PLESIOSAURS

Loch and Zaidee looked to the east corridor of the lake once the search fleet had passed. Finally, they saw a lone boat cutting through the water toward them. As it neared, they saw Sarah waving to them from behind the wheel of an old fishing skiff.

"See," Loch told Zaidee, "she comes through."

"I still don't trust her," Zaidee said through

her teeth. "Besides, it's just a dumpy old fishing boat."

"I think you should stay at the camp," Loch said.

"No way." Zaidee made a face.

"Zaidee," Loch said, "it really would be safer."

"Look," Zaidee said. "You can depend on me. I'm not going to let you risk your life with some daddy's little girl with no guts. She won't be there for you when you need her. She doesn't even like fish."

"You'll have nightmares."

"Wee Beastie needs me!" Zaidee stamped her foot.

Sarah threw the boat into neutral as she neared the dock. She let the momentum and wind glide the boat in. Loch grabbed the front tie rope while Zaidee jumped aboard.

"The boat's not very fast," Sarah apologized, "but at least it's bigger than your boat."

Loch recognized the skiff as he boarded and pushed off. "It was in the first day's search."

"Right. They dropped it out when they got the PT," Sarah said. "I had to take this or a twenty-seven-foot Seasprite with a leak."

Loch swung around into the open cabin and took over the wheel. He shifted into reverse. The dual propellers churned the water behind them, drawing the boat backward and away from the dock. At the edge of the black water, he shifted into forward and brought the boat around and headed across the lake.

"Where are we going?" Sarah asked.

"The logging camp."

"Why?"

Loch knew he had to warn them. "I found the caretaker's head last night," he said. "You don't want to know about that, but something's spilling the logs out of the pond there."

"You found Jesse Sanderson's head?" Zaidee said, her eyes wide. "Oh, puke."

"I'll give you the grisly details later. How fast does this baby go?" Loch asked.

"You saw me," Sarah said.

Loch threw the throttle full open. The motor roared, settling the rear of the skiff deeper into the water. It threw out an enormous wake and lifted the bow above the horizon line.

"It's doing ten, maybe twelve knots," Loch called over the noise. "That's not too bad."

"Glad you like it," Sarah said. She moved

closer to him, putting her arm around his waist.

Zaidee gagged. "Oh, that's cute."

"How would you know what's cute?" Sarah asked.

Zaidee stuck her tongue out and sat on the side bench. She started checking out the equipment on board. There was a coil of old rope, rusted trolling gear, and a half dozen tar-covered life vests in a center storage chest. She rummaged through the life vests, picked out the cleanest one, and put it on, tying the strings in front into neat bows. She moved forward to get a better look at the electronic equipment. There was a gaping hole in the center where the sonar equipment had been pulled out, but an old tuner protruded from the right of the control panel.

"At least they left the radio," Zaidee said.

Loch stayed on a course straight across the lake. He wanted to spend as little time as possible traveling in the deepest water, and at ten knots he figured no creature would have the time or the inclination to take a bead on them. If there was one thing he really believed about the beasts, it was that they wouldn't attack unless they thought someone was going to harm them.

"Careful in the shallows," Sarah said as the boat approached the north shore.

"Right," Loch said, circling wide to the left, then straightening the skiff out to run parallel along the deep-water line.

The three of them looked in awe at the huge wall of thick, tall pines that rose from the rocks of the north shore. The late-morning sun wasn't high enough yet in the sky to light the mammoth trees of the north bank. Farther up the shallows disappeared altogether, blending into a great blackness of water. From here the massive scars the logging mill had inflicted on the mountains could be glimpsed on the highest ridges.

Sarah pointed, shouting above the din of the motor: "There's the mill."

Zaidee was on her feet now, watching the approach to the boathouse with its long wooden dock. The mill itself was a long rectangle of corrugated tin, with an entire wall of windows overlooking the lake. It was cantilevered on jutting supports that thrust the building high out over the water. An elevated sluice emerged from one end of the building like the tracks of a roller coaster.

Zaidee felt a chill. "Jeez, it looks spooky."

"If Wee Beastie's anywhere, it's around here," Loch said.

At the base of the mill was the holding pond, its surface covered with enormous, moldering logs left over from when the mill had closed.

Loch took the boat in closer, checking the levee between the log pond and the lake. "That's where all the logs have been drifting out from," Loch said, pointing to a break in the levee. He shifted the boat into neutral, letting it glide toward the dock. Sarah took the wheel as Loch ran out on the bow and jumped onto the dock with the front tie rope. A second later Sarah jumped onto the dock and secured the rear tie.

"You stay with the boat," Loch told Zaidee.

"I don't want to," Zaidee complained.

"Just until Sarah and I check something out," Loch said. He reached over and smoothed Zaidee's hair, which, thanks to the wind, was standing up like the bristles of a brush. She looked at him pleadingly. "But you can depend on me. You need me. . . . "

"We'll be right back," Loch told her. "I promise."

Zaidee watched her brother and Sarah head down the dock toward the boathouse. "Five minutes!" she called after him. "Please find Wee Beastie!" Then she remembered the skiff's radio. She'd play with that awhile.

➤

"It's a nice little boathouse," Sarah said, looking up at the picture window on the second floor. "It's like the dwarfs' cottage in 'Snow White,'" she added. "My mom made Dad buy a new place in Switzerland. She hangs out there full-time now. It's got the same kind of boathouse, but with six boat slips underneath and a couple of heavy-duty racing boats. You've got to come over."

"Sometime when your father's not there," Loch said, checking the water on both sides of the dock.

"Exactly," Sarah said.

Closer, they saw the door to the boathouse had been left open. It swung gently in the breeze.

"Hello! Anybody here?" Loch called out. He knew Jesse wouldn't be showing up, but maybe he had some kind of family or friends.

Walking inside the boathouse, Loch and Sarah saw a small outboard and a canoe bobbing in their slips. "Anybody here?" Loch called again, his voice reverberating between the water and the second floor.

"Nobody's here," Sarah said.

They started up the steps to the living quarters. At the top of the stairs they heard a TV playing. Loch knocked on the door. There was no answer.

"This place is deserted," Loch said, reaching out turning the doorknob. The door was unlocked and they went in.

"Who'd go out on the lake and leave their TV on?" Sarah asked. "Unless you think the caretaker got it right here, of course."

"No," Loch said.

Sarah sat in the armchair in front of the TV. She grabbed the remote and started flipping through the channels. Loch went to the picture window to check on Zaidee. He had a clear view of her with a pair of earphones on her head in the boat at the end of the dock. She saw him and gave a big wave.

It was then that Loch noticed the motion of the water in front of the boathouse. It was as if a wave were forming, a slow surging of water heading into the open boat slips below. Loch shut the TV off.

"Hey, what are you doing?" Sarah asked.

Loch put a finger to his lips. "Shhhhhh," he whispered. "Something's here."

The small boathouse began to vibrate, and the blood drained from Sarah's face. She had felt that motion before on the catamaran with Erdon. . . .

➤

In black-rubber dive suits and scuba gear, Dr. Sam and Randolph climbed down the stern ladder to the rear swim platform of the yacht. Randolph steadied himself and motioned a crew member to pass down a speargun armed with an explosive head. He asked Dr. Sam to hold the speargun while he finished adjusting his equipment.

"Make sure Emilio signals us if anything comes back on the sonar," Randolph called up to the deck.

Cavenger's head peered down at him from

the top railing. "You're wasting time. Get in the water and fix the damn thing!"

Randolph put his mask and mouthpiece in place and rolled off the platform into the water. When he surfaced, Dr. Sam carefully placed the speargun in his hands. He waited until Randolph was good and clear, then put his own mask and mouthpiece in place. He turned on the dive lamp mounted on his back, then followed Randolph into the murky water.

Below the surface, Dr. Sam kicked his flippers to trail Randolph down the side of the hull. The powerful arc light bounced off the chalk-white paint of the ship's hull, giving them a visibility of nearly twenty feet. Clusters of peat particles rushed at his mask, and the aerator in his mouth turned his breathing into a pronounced wheezing. He felt unsure, all systems of his body on alert as if he were diving in shark waters.

Randolph reached the propeller first. Dr. Sam swam to his side, grasping the propeller-shaft cowling so he could hold the light steady. The edges of the prop were chipped, but this was nothing that would have stopped the ship. Randolph put the safety binding on the speargun, leaving both hands free. He moved his fingers to the base of the prop and signaled Dr. Sam to bring the light around. He set a grip plier onto a thick rod that looked like a large hairpin. The rod slid right out.

"Cotter pin's sheared," Randolph said, his voice distorted, bubbling through the water to Dr. Sam's ears.

Dr. Sam nodded that he understood, took a new pin from his waist kit, and handed it to Randolph. It slid in easily, and Randolph used the pliers to bend the ends of the pin and lock it into place.

"That's it," Randolph said.

Suddenly, both men became aware of a movement to the port side of the ship's under-belly. At first Dr. Sam thought it was some type of parallax effect from the arc light reflecting off their air tanks.

"Let's get out of here," Dr. Sam said, giving a thumbs-up signal.

Randolph signaled him to wait. He un-clipped the speargun and swam in the direction of the movement. There was another move-ment, this one to the starboard, followed by a glimpse of a small black body hurtling itself into the light field, then disappearing.

Dr. Sam signaled Randolph again that he was going up. He had started away from the center beam when he heard a high-pitched cry like that of a small land animal or seabird. Randolph began backing toward Dr. Sam, as two more small creatures darted in and out at the edge of the light beam. The only frame of reference Dr. Sam had for such animal behavior was on the few occasions he had swum with very young seals and penguins.

"Come on," Dr. Sam said.

"Wait," Randolph insisted.

Another of the little creatures came fast by Randolph, then scooted quickly to disappear out into the blackness again. Randolph got a good look at it this time and knew it was smaller than the creature that had been with the kids when he and his men had chased them in the grid. It was younger, maybe only days old. His mind began to spin with the possibilities of how Cavenger would reward him if he could bring the carcass of one up to *The Revelation*.

"By God, I'll go up without you," Dr. Sam threatened, reaching out to Randolph's shoulder to turn him.

"No," Randolph said.

If there was one thought creeping into Dr. Sam's head, it was the realization that there was a family of plesiosaurs in the lake, maybe as many as eight or ten, including the young ones.

The creatures' cries grew more piercing, excited now. Randolph shook off Dr. Sam's hand and raised his speargun.

"No," Dr. Sam yelled, the air of his shout bursting out to block the view beyond his mask. When the bubbles cleared he saw a few of the creatures flying at them, each on a slightly different trajectory like atomic particles in a cloud chamber.

Randolph let loose the spear.

The spear sped forward beyond the light before it struck something. The explosion from its tip was small, a slight shock wave of sound and light.

Dr. Sam thought about hitting Randolph, about putting his arm around his neck and physically dragging him up to the surface.

The cries stopped.

Randolph smiled at Dr. Sam. Then he signaled that he was swimming forward under the hull to retrieve the specimen. Randolph got only a few yards before the cries returned, this time in a rush that was earsplitting. There was only a moment to be aware of the painful, angry sounds, before five of the small creatures flew straight at Randolph. They hurtled themselves at him like missiles, their cartilage-rimmed mouths opening to reveal the gums of their jaws and their oversized, needlelike teeth. Like a school of piranha they struck Randolph's body, first tearing away dozens of small pieces of his rubber suit and then, finally, his flesh.

Dr. Sam started to swim toward Randolph to drag him away from the creatures. But the wounds were too deep now. Blood streamed out into the water as if from punctures in a large, struggling doll. Finally, as the creatures pulled their attacker down, deeper, away from the light, one of Randolph's arms was bitten free of his body.

The last Dr. Sam saw of Randolph was the halo of creatures surrounding his head like a scarlet wreath as they plunged him into darkness.

IN THE CUTTING ROOM

The vibrations from beneath the boathouse grew stronger. Sarah froze in the armchair, looking to Loch to see what their next move would be. They heard Zaidee calling to them from the end of the dock.

From the picture window Loch saw her still wearing the radio earphones in the boat. She was waving at him. "Hey! Something's happened on *The Revelation*! I can hear what they're radioing," she shouted.

Loch wanted to cry out to Zaidee, to warn her—but he didn't dare make a sound. Somehow he felt the creatures would know she meant them no harm.

"Dad's quit!" Zaidee shouted happily. "Cavenger wants him off the boat immediately. I think a helicopter's lifting him back to the base. . . . "

Zaidee's voice suddenly cracked and she went silent. Loch watched her lift her hand and point toward the boat slips beneath him. She was seeing something he couldn't. All at once Sarah's and Loch's eyes opened in terror as the monstrous head of the Rogue lifted into view, filling the frame of the window. The massive yellow eyes of the beast fixed upon them behind the glass.

Sarah screamed as the shadow fell over her.

"Don't move!" Loch told her, but she was out of control. She leaped up from the chair. Her hand reached out, and she grabbed a heavy ashtray from the table.

"No!" Loch shouted, rushing toward her—but it was too late.

Sarah hurled the ashtray toward the Rogue.

CRASH.

The picture window exploded. The Rogue shook his head, startled by the attack. He let out a loud, shrieking blast from his nostrils, slime splattering across the living room as he thrust his head forward.

The head and neck of a second beast, its snout thinner, coarser, ripped up through the center of the floor, blocking the door through which they had entered. Loch spotted another door, one off the kitchen. He grabbed Sarah's hand.

"Go!" Loch yelled, pushing Sarah ahead of him.

In a moment they were out the door, running up the stairs of a breezeway. They burst through yet another door into a huge, empty warehouse with high, vaulted ceilings of corrugated tin.

"Where are we?" Sarah cried out, her heart pounding in her chest.

Loch looked at the cluster of machinery and huge blades at the far end of the building. "I think it's the cutting room," he said.

CRASH. The entire building shook.

Loch remembered the building was can-tilevered out over the lake. "The creatures are hitting the supports."

There was another, stronger impact near the breezeway, this time with the sound of metal twisting, beams cracking.

"Come on," Loch yelled, grabbing Sarah's hand and running for the far end of the build-ing. Daylight streamed in through the cracks of what looked like a barn door past the huge saw-ing machinery. They swung the doors open, only to see a narrow walkway onto the elevated log sluice.

CRASH. The entire building trembled, began to dip downward, shattering the wall of windows. The only way out was onto the sluice.

"I hate heights!" Sarah shouted to Loch as he led her out and along the rickety gully. On both sides of the sluice was a fifty-foot drop.

There was another shock to the building, and a wall of logs on the mountain began to waken.

Loch looked back as the sound of the low, frightening rumble began to grow. There was a rush of water onto the sluice, and one by one logs dropped into the flow. The first log hurtled toward them.

"We're going to have to jump into the log pond," Loch said.

"I'm not jumping anywhere," Sarah yelled.

"Get ready!" Loch warned, holding her hand firmly.

"I'm not jumping."

"Yes, you are!"

Loch leaped, taking Sarah with him. They dropped down, down into the slim wedge of open water at the rim of the log pond, and surfaced quickly. For a moment they thought they were safe, but there came a rumbling noise from above.

"Oh, my God!" Sarah cried, as they looked up to see the sluice breaking and a log hurtling down at them. It fell with all the speed and force of a huge battering ram. Loch grabbed Sarah, set his feet against a pylon, and pushed them both away. The falling log crashed into the water next to them, a single untrimmed branch tearing across Loch's shoulder like a whip.

"You're bleeding," Sarah gasped as they

pulled themselves up onto the nearest floating log.

"It's nothing," Loch said, standing. Beyond the levee of the log pond, he saw, Zaidee was at the wheel of the skiff.

"Come on!" Zaidee yelled.

Loch waved to Zaidee and helped Sarah to her feet.

"Where are the monsters?" Sarah called to Zaidee across the landscape of logs.

"They were heading for you!" Zaidee yelled back.

Sarah's eyes dropped. She saw the logs at the edge of the pond begin rising and falling.

"Let's go," Loch said, leaping forward onto the next log in the jam.

WHOOSH. A large plesiosaur rose out of the water behind Sarah. Its neck pulled back, its mouth opened wide. Sarah leaped toward Loch.

"Keep moving!" Loch ordered Sarah, pushing her on to the next log. By the time the creature lunged, they were running on top of the logs for all they were worth. Its teeth snapped at air; then it slid back beneath the surface.

"Hurry!" Zaidee screamed to them, nudging

the bow of the skiff against the bank.

Suddenly, the log beneath Sarah started to lift up into the air. She fell across it and hung on as it balanced crazily on the massive head of a beast. The beast's left front flipper crashed out of the water, slapping on top of another log to give it leverage. Loch ran straight for the creature as it raised its snout and thrust its lower bed of teeth forward. The rotting log with Sarah on it began to slide off the beast's head. Loch tore off a branch and smashed it against the creature's fin. The beast snapped at Loch, its teeth locking on the branch, cracking it into specks. The sudden motion set the creature off balance, and its fin slipped from the log. As the beast's own weight pulled it back under, Loch grabbed Sarah and ran forward with her across the final stretch of logs to the bank of the levee and the awaiting boat.

Zaidee was ready at the controls.

"I take it all back," Zaidee told Sarah as she helped her onto the boat. "You *do* have guts."

"Thanks," Sarah said, collapsing into the boat. "You have guts, too."

THE
JUDGMENT

Cavenger had been glad when the helicopter had arrived to remove Dr. Sam from the yacht and take him back to the encampment. You don't win the Grand Prix by stopping if someone crashes, Cavenger had to remind everyone. While all the other drivers are feeling bad about the flames and the wreckage and the burning corpse, that's when you floor it!

"What should we do now?" Emilio asked Cavenger when the fleet had finished the sweep of the lake.

Cavenger swiveled in his seat at the control

board. "We start back, sonar active."

Emilio transmitted the order to the fleet. Captain Haskell led the turnaround at the west end of the lake. The fishing trawlers clanked their way past each other in a wide semicircle, giving great berth to the nets and exchanging flank positions for the return search. Cavenger motioned Emilio to keep his eye on the sonar screens, got up, and went to the munitions chest. He lifted the lid to check the rocket launcher and grenades. If any creature came their way now, Cavenger wanted everyone ready for a kill.

➤

On the skiff, Loch took over the wheel and threw the throttle open. The propellers growled, pulling the stern deeper and lifting the bow as the skiff began to plow out toward the open lake. A hundred yards away from the levee, Zaidee spotted a small, sleek, black shape darting in and out of their wake.

"Stop!" Zaidee yelled. "It's Wee Beastie!"

Loch turned, saw the creature, and cut the throttle. He shifted into neutral and rushed to the stern.

"It's really not a great time to be saying hello

to our little plesiosaur friend, you know," Sarah said. Loch and Zaidee hung over the rear railing as Wee Beastie scuttled through the remnants of the wake and swam right up to the boat.

"Hey, fellah," Loch said, reaching his hand down toward the water. Wee Beastie rubbed his snout on Loch's hand, fluttering his front fins.

"Where have you been, my little darlin'?" Zaidee leaned over, joyously stroking the creature's head. "We've been looking for you!"

CLACK CLICK . . .

CLICK CLACK CLACK . . .

"Don't tell me, I know," Sarah said. "He wants us to stay and be lunch."

CLACK CLICK . . .

"What are you trying to tell us?" Loch asked Wee Beastie.

Loch looked back at the twisted mill. A series of large waves flowed toward the rupture in the levee and out into the lake.

"They're coming out," Loch said.

"We've got to get Wee Beastie aboard," Zaidee cried.

"Zaidee," Loch said, "I don't think his mom's really going to like that. Besides, there isn't time."

CLICK CLACK CLICK . . .

Loch pointed Wee Beastie to the starboard. "Move away from the props, fellah!" he yelled as he rushed back to the wheel. Wcc Beastie scooted back, still clicking away as the disturbance in the water behind them got nearer.

"Get us out of here!" Sarah shouted at Loch.

Loch opened the throttle wide, and the skiff lunged forward.

"He's staying with us," Zaidee yelled, watching Wee Beastie drop away from the gurgling props to dash in and out of the wake. Behind him the turbulence of the surface stalked them.

"Uh-oh," Zaidee said.

"How many creatures are there?" Sarah asked.

Loch turned from the wheel to look back. "From what we've seen, I think there's five or six big ones," he shouted. "I think it's just a family."

"Enough to eat Greater Miami," Zaidee said.

"What are they doing?" Sarah wanted to know.

"They're not stupid," Loch yelled over the roar of the engine. "They know the cover's been blown on their den. There's no place left for them to hide!" He turned the skiff west. Wee Beastie and the herd stayed with them.

"Are we the only meal around?" Sarah asked.

"No," Loch said, "but Wee Beastie might have told them we're their only chance. They're not chasing us—they're following us."

"What can we do?" Zaidee asked.

"Try to get Dad on the ship-to-shore," Loch said.

"I don't know if I can," Zaidee said, scooting to the radio. "It receives, but I don't know if this thing can send." She put the earphones on and grabbed the hand mike. "The helicopter took him back to the camp."

"He'd clear out of there. Try the Volvo," Loch said. "Let him know where we are and what's happening."

"Boy, are we going to be grounded or what?" Zaidee wailed, pressing the send button.

"I'll do it," Sarah said, reaching to take the mike.

"No way," Zaidee said, pulling away and

shouting into the microphone. "Big Z to Dad . . . Big Z to Dad . . ."

Loch glanced over his shoulder. Wee Beastie still skimmed in the wake of the boat, leading the underwater herd.

"Tell Dad to get to the grid! Get there and open it!" Loch ordered Zaidee. "He's got to open that grid!"

➤

"What's that?" Cavenger shouted, looking out over the bow of *The Revelation*. In the distance it had looked like a cat's-paw of wind, but now they recognized the skiff heading for them.

"It's one of ours," Emilio said, checking it through binoculars.

"Who's in it?" Cavenger demanded to know.

Emilio adjusted the focus on the binoculars. "Your daughter and Perkins' kids."

BLIP BLIP . . . BLIP BLIP . . .

The sonar screens of the control room leaped alive with closing, black dots. A rush of electronic sounds caused turmoil with the speakers, and the styluses on the graph machines nearly shot off the charts.

"What's going on!" Cavenger roared,

grabbing the binoculars. "What the hell do those kids think they're doing?"

The radio receiver lit up. "Everybody's picking up the signals," Emilio said, confused. "It's the boat, but it's . . . beasts. There are a lot of them."

"Tell the net boats to close!" Cavenger roared.

"Close the nets!" Emilio shouted into the radio.

"Faster," Cavenger yelled, moving quickly across the length of the control console.

BLIP . . . BLIP . . .

There was too much data coming in for Cavenger and his men to process, too much to compute and calculate. The trawlers were pulling ahead, beginning to close their circle. Cavenger grabbed the mike out of Emilio's hand and began bellowing into it himself. "Faster! Faster!"

"They're doing as much as they can," Emilio said.

BLIP . . .

Cavenger threw the mike back at Emilio. "They're not going to make it!" he shouted with disgust. All his calculations had never considered the possibility of the fleet being rushed by a herd of plesiosaurs. He looked off the port side and was relieved to see the crew members of the PT boat ready with rifle butts held firmly against their shoulders. The new photographer—who hadn't been told about Erdon—was at the video camera, following the action. Cavenger checked to see that the harpoon team was in position at the bow, then grabbed a pistol and ran out on deck. The skiff with Loch at the wheel passed swiftly between the yacht and the PT boat. Cavenger saw his daughter with Loch and Zaidee. And he saw the great undulations fast behind them.

He fired a single shot into the air to alert everyone. There was no way he was going to come out of this empty-handed. If anything, he would err on overkill.

"Slaughter the beasts!" he found himself shouting, his hand trembling as he pointed down at the huge passing shadows. "Slaughter them!"

➢

As Sarah passed in the skiff, she saw her father out on the deck of *The Revelation*. She didn't recognize him at first; his face was distorted with hate and he looked out of control. She had never seen him like that, and she flinched when she heard him fire the gun.

"What's going to happen?" Sarah asked Loch.

"I don't know," Loch said. "We have to keep going."

"What if Dad didn't hear us on the ship-to-shore?" Zaidee asked. "What if he didn't understand or *won't* open the grid?"

BAM. BAM. BAM . . .

Terrible sounds of rifle fire echoed from the mountains like a cluster of firecrackers lit from a single fuse.

"Where's Wee Beastie?" Zaidee cried out. "I don't see him!"

"My father's killing them," Sarah said.

Loch looked back, reading the surface of the water. "No," he said, "they're running deep now. The bullets won't get them. I'm sure Wee Beastie's okay."

Loch glanced to the south shore at a point where the paved road weaved for a stretch close to the lake. If only Dr. Sam had heard their radio plea, if only they would catch a glimpse of the Volvo speeding along the road toward the end of the lake and the grid.

BAM!

The shooting started again as *The Revelation* and the PT boat turned about quickly and took up pursuit. The rest of the fleet floundered, struggling to turn and re-form.

Zaidee was the first to see the little, black, shining body skimming again through the wake of their skiff.

"Wee Beastie!" she shouted happily.

The Revelation was gaining on them, the PT boat pacing itself easily off its port.

Loch saw the grid and its cement control bunker in the distance. He searched the ridge for any glimpse of his father. There was no one.

"The plesiosaurs are surfacing!" Zaidee cried out.

Loch looked back to see the water rupture as the creatures' dark, scaly backs began to emerge from the lake. Their speed slowed and the handful of smaller beasts began to panic, skimming to the surface at the edges of the adults like frightened fish. Only one huge head began to rise from the herd, the tremendous bony mass and snout of the Rogue. The Rogue slowed, dropping back like a patriarch whose instincts are clear.

"What is the Rogue doing?" Zaidee asked.

Loch, understanding what was happening, answered sadly. "Protecting his family."

The Revelation closed the distance between itself and the Rogue. Cavenger and his team were in place at the bow, the harpooner manning the huge gun. The Rogue lifted his head higher, showing more of his neck and letting the yacht come within striking distance.

"Oh, God, please don't . . . " Sarah said aloud, as if magic would carry her words to her father. As much as she feared the beasts, she didn't want to see them destroyed like this.

BOOM.

The first harpoon exploded from the gun and entered the Rogue's neck so deeply its shiny, metal tip burst from the scales beneath his jaw. Blood spurted out of the wound, rushing down into the water of the lake as the creature snapped his neck back and forth, trying to break free.

BOOM.

Another harpoon tore into the Rogue's

shoulder, this one setting deep. Its explosive head detonated, blasting loose a vast slab of the creature's flesh and muscle.

The PT boat began to circle the beast, its crew firing and refiring rifles, pumping bullets into his body. Sarah put her hands to her ears to try to block out the terrible, terrible noise of the shooting and the tortured roars of the beast. The Rogue kept trying to turn his head as if to see whether his herd was safe.

"The creatures are passing us," Zaidee yelled as the clear springs of the shallows replaced the darker peat water.

She watched the huge blackness of the beasts rush by beneath them to halt at the mouth of the grid. What might have been Beast and two of the other larger plesiosaurs surfaced in front of the boat, forcing Loch to cut the motor and shift into neutral.

"They're going to eat us!" Sarah screamed, flashes of what had happened to Erdon stabbing back into her mind.

"They could have done that already," Loch said, ready at the wheel for anything.

With the skiff stopped, the herd had strangely quieted, the creatures sinking to the bottom. Only Wee Beastie stayed off the boat's stern, clicking at them, motioning with his snout toward the slaughter of the Rogue, as if there were something they could do.

"What's going on?" Zaidee asked, confused.

They looked back at *The Revelation*. Perhaps in a last desperate attempt to escape, the Rogue had sounded in the deep water. The harpoons were holding, their lines drawn taut as the yacht began to list from the great weight and strength of the beast.

Cavenger pushed his way to the railing and stared down into the black and bloodied water. Emilio, with a belt of grenades, appeared at his side.

"Kill it!" Cavenger screamed at him. "Kill it now!"

Emilio took a grenade, pulled its pin, and hurled it down into the water. Seconds later, there was the great sickening thud of an under-water blast and a great fountain of blood and water erupted from the surface of the lake. Still the harpoon lines were taut, pulling the boat down.

"Throw another grenade!" Cavenger ordered.

Emilio had time only to draw the pin out before the Rogue suddenly shot up out of the water like a huge submarine surfacing from a great depth. His body angled across the bow, then came crashing down and ripped away a section of the hull. He slashed forward with his fins as the men with guns on the PT blasted him mercilessly. One of the better marksmen hit the beast's left eye, bursting it.

The impact of the Rogue's attack caused Emilio to drop the live grenade on the deck. Cavenger saw the grenade fall, then watched helplessly as it rolled back, past the crew, and dropped into the maze of cables and wires of the sonar power base.

"It's going to blow!" Emilio shouted, diving over the side.

Cavenger's first, completely absurd, impulse was to berate Emilio, to scold and blame him for not following orders precisely. The harpoon team pushed by him, heading for the railing. The rest of the crew ran for the stern. In these last, futile seconds, Cavenger had no one left to order, no one to command. He was standing alone when the Rogue's head snapped toward him. The mouth opened and the huge vise of teeth slowly closed on Cavenger's head. In a paroxysm of death, the creature jerked back his neck, lifting Cavenger into the burning sun of a tremendous explosion.

Sarah screamed and threw up her hands to cover her face as a second, greater blast swallowed *The Revelation* in an immense ball of fire. As the storm of smoke and flames rose up into the sky, Loch went to Sarah and put his arm around her.

"I'm sorry," Loch said gently. "I'm very sorry."

The fireball turned into streaks of black and raining embers as the remnants of the hull began to slide beneath the surface of the lake. When Sarah lowered her hands from her eyes, her entire body shuddered and she burst into tears. "He was my father . . . my father," she cried. "I know he didn't always do the right thing—he needed so much to prove to everyone he was right. . . ."

"I guess being right isn't enough," Loch said, looking up to the desolate ridge. "I don't think it was enough for any of us."

Zaidee rushed to Sarah, flung her arms around her, and began to cry too.

CLICK CLICK . . .

They heard the sounds, and saw Wee Beastie's head peer over the stern at them. He looked at them for only a moment, then swam slowly down to the herd.

Lake Alban was silent. A few of the crew from *The Revelation* had survived the great, ripping blast and had managed to swim to the PT. The crews of the fleet stood quietly on their decks, all guns pointed toward the skiff with the beasts beneath it.

Loch was the first to hear the sounds from below. "They're making their music," he said.

"Why?" Sarah asked.

The water around the skiff began to stir, then churn. It moved in increasingly greater swirls and turmoil until the heads and bodies of the beasts began to rise all about them. The beasts surfaced in a great circle, their heads and necks lifting high above the boat.

Loch, Sarah, and Zaidee stood together, looking up at the leviathans. The sound they made now was like that of a thousand cellos, a series of low, haunting notes that slid upward into an increasingly profound and complicated harmony. The music of the plesiosaurs was penetrating, vibrating the air in a way that could be felt on the skin and in the heart. Their singing transcended words and even thoughts, as Loch felt a warmth start in his brain, then move down his spine and flood his entire body. He knew from the look in Zaidee's and Sarah's eyes that they were feeling it, too.

To a man, the men with guns lowered their weapons as the sounds swept over them.

Loch didn't know how he knew, but suddenly he was certain his father was on the ridge. He looked to the cement control bunker. Zaidee's eyes followed his. They saw Dr. Sam looking down at them.

"Will Dad open the grid?" Zaidee asked.

"Yes," Loch said.

Dr. Sam waved to them. He knew what had to be done, and he unlocked the door of the bunker. Inside, he punched the code into the controls. In seconds the hydraulics of the grid came alive. Still singing, the beasts slowly sank beneath the surface of the lake as the grid parted its massive gates. There was a tremendous surge of water as the river was restored to its full depth, and the beasts slowly swam into the rush of water flowing toward

Lake Champlain—toward their home.

CLICK CLICK.

Only Wee Beastie surfaced. He remained off the stern of the skiff, his eyes glowing at them.

"He wants to stay with us," Zaidee cried out.

"I think he does," Loch said, "but he knows he can't."

Wee Beastie lifted his snout and shook it at them. Zaidee rushed forward to pet him. She looked closely into the creature's eyes and knew her brother was right.

"Good-bye, Wee Beastie," Zaidee cried out. "Good-bye!"

The light in Wee Beastie's eyes slowly faded. He shook his snout again, turned, and dug his fins hard and deep toward the open grid to follow the song of the plesiosaurs.

Dr. Sam waved to his kids from the knoll.

"We're a family again, aren't we?" Zaidee asked Loch as she waved back.

"You bet we are," Loch said, holding Sarah close to him. A wide grin broke out across his face as he lifted his hand into the air. "We're a family."

PAUL ZINDEL, author of such teen favorites as *The Pigman* and *Pardon Me, You're Stepping on My Eyeball!*, along with many more, has won numerous awards, including the Pulitzer Prize in drama for *The Effect of Gamma Rays on Man-in-the-Moon Marigolds.*

A nonreader himself until later in life, Zindel writes books for kids who don't like to read. A former high school chemistry teacher, he draws upon his scientific background for *Loch.* Zindel lives in New York City.